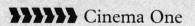

15 Samuel Fuller

Samuel Fuller

Nicholas Garnham

The Viking Press
New York

The Cinema One Series is published by The Viking Press, Inc., in
association with *Sight and Sound* and the Education Department of
the British Film Institute

Published in 1972 in a hardbound and paperbound edition by
The Viking Press, Inc.
625 Madison Avenue, New York, N.Y. 10022

SBN 670–61663–X (hardbound)
    670–01925–9 (paperbound

Library of Congress catalog number: 75–173870

Printed and bound in Great Britain

Contents

Cover: Fuller on location for Dennis Hopper's *The Last Movie*

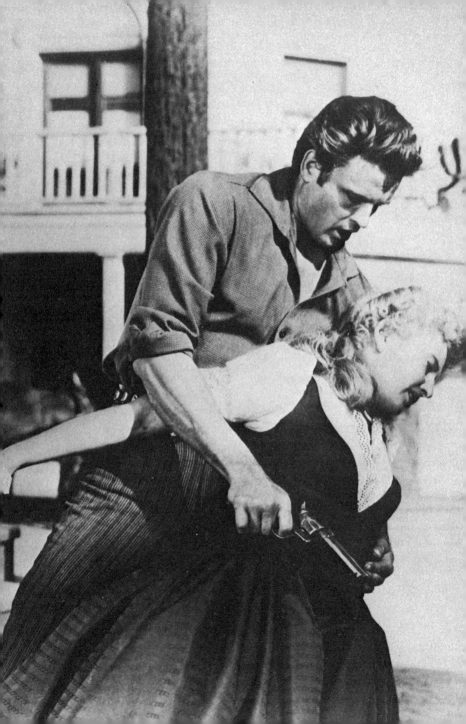

Introduction

'I don't agree that criticism is indispensable. It's easy to criticize and I believe that Chopin, Rodin or Tolstoy would have done exactly what they did without criticism, and that Beethoven would have left as rich a legacy. I have a book on the correspondence between H. G. Wells and Henry James. It's extraordinary but at that level it's not really criticism. For instance, one of them would find something in the other's work which would make him exclaim: "Yes you're right!"' (Fuller)

I must make clear right from the start what kind of criticism this book contains. Just as Fuller's movies are not cool and objective, so this book does not contain cool, objective criticism. You will find here none of that 'on the one hand, on the other hand' sort of criticism which handles its subject from a distance, criticism which reminds me of those remote-controlled arms they use in laboratories for handling radio-active substances, criticism moreover that both implies the superiority of critic over film-maker and makes you wonder how the critic sat through the film at all. I am concerned here not to administer admonitory raps on Fuller's cinematic knuckles, but to exclaim and I hope cause others to exclaim 'Yes, you're right!'

This book is a labour of love, a love born in the dark womb of Sunday afternoon moviehouses in rain-drenched provincial towns and the seedier areas of London. This book is the culmination of an odyssey whose islands are ancient cinemas named Rex, Imperial, Tolmer, whose sirens are named Fuller, Boetticher, Siegel, Ray, Mann and Aldrich. To see in those half-empty moviehouses, smelling of damp clothes and nicotine, above the heads of sheltering old-age pensioners the images of *House of Bamboo*, *Pickup on South Street* or *Merrill's Marauders* was to come face to face with a

7

Forty Guns : the death of Jessica (Barbara Stanwyck)

cinematic presence that demanded recognition. This book records the process of that recognition.

Fuller has always worked in the mainstream of American commercial cinema and yet his *œuvre* can be assimilated into a European tradition of authorship more easily than that of any other major American director. The credit 'Written, Produced and Directed by Samuel Fuller' is unique in modern Hollywood cinema. It is an explicit claim to total authorship shared only by Orson Welles and Joseph Mankiewicz. So in Fuller's case it should not be necessary to enter the incessant controversy that surrounds the *auteur* theory. All apparently that is necessary is an evaluation of the movies. But paradoxically it is just such a view of the privileged artist and the self-contained work of art that Fuller's movies, and therefore this book, are concerned to reject.

In this book I study not individual movies, but a total work. As Renoir has said, movie directors are really creating one long movie for which each individual movie is a sequence. Only when the last movie is finished can the whole *œuvre* be fully understood. It is like a house that doesn't make sense until the roof is on. One hopes Fuller has not yet finished making movies, and this book, like all good criticism, must inevitably be tentative. However, many critics find it hard to accept this view that one should be concerned with the *œuvre* rather than with the individual movie. The concept of the isolated, self-contained artefact dies hard. But one accepts surely that any movie is only part of a continuum of human experience. We none of us come wholly innocent to any experience. If we were not allowed to refer outside the work of art being criticized, criticism would be impossible; the experience would remain unique and incommunicable. But of course criticism depends upon reference to numerous structures of common knowledge, aesthetics, ethics, politics, history, etc. What one is asking here is that the whole work of the author should be recognized, not only as one of these structures, but as the one nearest and perhaps most relevant to the matter in hand. The

8

concept of the single, inviolate work of art is proper only to a religious age, for it is really an attempt at immortality. Once one accepts evolution, relativity, the idea of historical flow, the lonely masterpiece becomes an anachronism, stranded and almost meaningless, like the huge feet in Shelley's *Ozymandias*.

A movie takes place, as Godard has pointed out, not on the screen but in the space between the screen and the audience. We are an essential part of any movie. As we are changed by our environment, so the movie changes. It floats free from whoever created it. As Lawrence wrote in *Studies in Classic American Literature*: 'Art-speech is the only truth. An artist is usually a damned liar, but his art, if it be art, will tell you the truth of his day. And that is all that matters. Away with eternal truth.' Fuller recognizes the non-existence of eternal truth by, in many cases, giving his movies no ending. *The Steel Helmet* ends with the title 'This story has no end.' *Run of the Arrow* ends on the title 'The end of this story will be written by you.' Even when Fuller does not actually spell it out, his movies frequently end on an unresolved note. *Underworld USA* ends with us wondering whether Cuddles will sing on Smith and therefore whether 'Tolly died for nothing'. The resolution will come in the future, beyond the movie itself. *Verboten* ends suddenly in the midst of a raging fire. And so in this book I do not discuss Fuller's work movie by movie in what is I suppose the conventional fashion. I do not attempt an assessment of any individual movie. His most completely successful movies in the conventional self-contained sense are, I suppose, *Pickup on South Street*, *Run of the Arrow*, *Merrill's Marauders* and *Underworld USA*. In general it is these movies that random viewers of Fuller's work prefer. They are the ones that most critics find it easier to approach. But, fine as they are, they would not by themselves convince me that Fuller was one of the major creative talents in the contemporary cinema.

I am not concerned to evaluate even the structural Fuller

Fuller during the shooting of *Verboten*; and in his Hollywood study

movie that contains the single Fuller movies within it. This book is not a work of evaluation so much as of elucidation. To write on Fuller is to venture into almost unexplored territory. There is little opportunity for the 'Yes, but' process of Leavisite criticism. *Cahiers du Cinéma* has bracketed Fuller with Kazan and Welles as the most significant directors of their generation, but there is little weight of critical evidence in the pages of the magazine to support this evaluation. In a generation that includes Nicholas Ray, Joseph Mankiewicz, Joseph Losey and Otto Preminger, such a claim is rash, even if one gives the word 'significant' a social connotation and equates significance with those Big Subjects *à la* Kramer that Chabrol attacked in *Cahiers* itself. But in the context of Kazan and Welles it is clearly just such an equation that is meant.

Raymond Durgnat has written that *Kiss Me Deadly* is not important because it tells us about Aldrich, but Aldrich is important because of what *Kiss Me Deadly* tells us about America. The problem is more complex than that. In a way it is by telling us about himself that a director tells us about America or France or Czechoslovakia or wherever. It is also true that if he were merely telling us about America his importance and significance, especially to non-Americans, would be limited. But it remains true that Fuller, like Aldrich, is important for what he tells us about America. The United States is central to our society and our culture, as a frontier for us all. It is a country set up as a political, social and cultural test-bed where we see acted out to their limits certain of the possibilities for the rest of us. It is still our New World and our future. I don't mean by this that we are destined to follow in America's footsteps. There are, as we are beginning to realize, other test-beds, other frontiers – China, Cuba, Czecho-slovakia. But the United States remains the most potent, and even if the dream is turning into a nightmare that nightmare is part of the experiment and part of our experience.

The movies are part of that web of language which defines our culture. To listen to that language is to understand in part how and why we live. Everything that is said is significant, an expression of ourselves. The channels that lead to an understanding of that significance are manifold. I have chosen a channel that can be identified as Samuel Fuller. He is, if you like, the nucleus round which a molecule of more general meaning is structured. But by choosing this particular channel I do not thereby deny the validity of others. It may well be possible to draw as much meaning out of an analysis of the iconographical significance of Richard Widmark, or by comparing all the movies made about the Korean War. My choice of Fuller, therefore, as the subject of a book establishes not so much a value judgement as a point of view. That point of view I regard as valuable, because I find that I can see a great deal from it.

For me, going to the movies is like going to a party. Some of the people I meet there I don't like, some become close friends. My friends I admire as much for their faults as their virtues. For the record I find *The Baron of Arizona* uncharacteristically dull and *Hell and High Water* almost unwatchable. (The latter movie, I think, demonstrates one of the traps of the *auteur* theory. The Fuller themes appear very clearly just because Fuller is not working on them with full creative power. They are just baldly stated.) But I don't love Fuller any the less for these lapses, for they remain movies that could have been made by no one else and they throw light on the unifying creative personality. Fuller, like Norman Mailer, puts his work before you, warts and all, take it or leave it. His movies to date are An Advertisement for Samuel Fuller, though this should not be taken to imply self-conscious pretentiousness. The refreshing thing about Fuller, a sign of his creative health, is that this book will give him a good laugh. Of course movie-making is more important than criticism, or rather it is the highest form of criticism. But I beg Fuller's indulgence and ask him to remember what his good friend Fritz Lang once said: 'I think a critic should be a kind of psychoanalyst who analyses the script a director has done and tells me why I make certain things. Because I know naturally why I do them, but I don't know the deeper reason for it. And only a psychoanalyst could tell me that.'

1 : Fuller's Kind of Cinema

'A painter, you know straight away whether he has any talent or not. He doesn't need to come and tell you that he's a painter and he's talented, you just have to look at his paintings.' (Fuller)

Fuller began his career as a journalist: at the age of fourteen he became a copy-boy on the *New York Journal* and by the age of seventeen he was one of the leading crime reporters in the States. He still regards himself primarily as a writer; his films are always yarns. As he said of *Shock Corridor*, 'It is full of front page material'. His films are extensions of his journalism; to understand them it is necessary to examine his attitudes to the fourth estate. These are embodied in *Park Row*, one of his finest films and the one he claims satisfied him most both emotionally and artistically. It was a film into which he put literally everything – it was his first independent production and he used his own money, a very rare sign of commitment in the movie industry. 'My favourite film is the greatest flop of all time, not just a flop, but the great flop. It was *Park Row* – I loved that project so much I financed it myself. At that time I had some money in the bank, exactly $201,000. I left 1,000 in the bank for cigars, brandy and vodka, I took the other 200,000 and put them in the film.' While shooting the film his camera-man lined up an exterior shot that didn't show the top of the buildings on the set he had constructed. Fuller turned to him and said: 'Let's get the top of the buildings in shot, that's my money up there.'

The central character of *Park Row* is Phineas Mitchell: 'In my story I wanted one character to combine all the great newspaper editors of the period. I took James Gordon Bennett of the *New York Herald*, Horace Greeley of the *Tribune*, Charles E. Dana of the *New York Sun* and the *Tribune*, Henry Smith of the *New York Times*, and Joseph Pulitzer of the *World*.' But above all Mitchell stands for Joseph Pulitzer, who, like the character in the film, collected money to erect the Statue of Liberty. Fuller establishes a close connection in the film between liberty and freedom of the Press. The second shot of the film shows the statue of Benjamin Franklin presiding over Park Row, as both America's first great journalist and printer, and also one of the signatories of the Declaration of Independence. In the long tracking crane shot that is the movie's title shot we see Phineas Mitchell walking along Park Row from beneath the shadow of the inspiration of Ben Franklin to the bar, where he will make his decision to fight for truth and integrity, whatever the personal cost.

That this decision should take place in a bar is important. In *Park Row* there are three interior sets: a bar, the offices of the *Star*, and the offices of the *Globe*. The *Star* is an established paper that combines respectability with muckraking. Phineas Mitchell starts the movie as a journalist on the staff of the *Star* but when he denounces an injustice (he thinks the *Star* has condemned a man to death just to sell newspapers) his boss, Miss Charity Hackett, sacks him. Throughout the movie the *Star* represents hypocrisy and is associated with established society, big business and the government. The bar is the home of the people: Miss Hackett comes into it as an intruder. It is here that Mitchell is given the chance to start an honest crusading newspaper, the *Globe*, and it is here that he recruits his staff and gets his first story. For Fuller the significance of the Statue of Liberty is that it was donated by a people to a people, not by a government to a government.

Bars, drink and art are connected elsewhere in Fuller's work. In *The Crimson Kimono* Mac the painter is an alcoholic whose work can be seen 'in the best bars and brothels on Skid Row'. Her art is equated with Fuller's. They both share the

Writing *Park Row*

same setting and the same concerns. Mac, like Moe in *Pickup on South Street*, is an informer. She reveals truths. This she can only do because she is fully involved with the seamy side of life. She rightly diagnoses the weakness of Chris's art as due to lack of experience. This view of the artist is another aspect of Fuller's reiterated contention that society is saved by its outcasts. The artist, like the journalist, is a more self-conscious version of the Fuller outsider, the rebel as a hero.

In *The Naked Kiss* Grant gives Kelly an ancient Venetian drinking goblet, a symbol of his identification with traditional European high-art. One is reminded of Henry James's *Golden Bowl*. When Kelly is trying to make up her mind whether to marry Grant she gets drunk on whisky from this goblet. We are aware of the clash between the sensitive, cultured living represented by the goblet and Kelly's hard, coarse prostitute's past represented by the whisky. Drink is repeatedly associated with prostitution in the movie, both through the Angel Foam Champagne Kelly peddles as a cover and through the bar across the river which is a front for a brothel. The complex morality of the movie depends upon us realizing that it is the whisky which represents health and the goblet perversion.

Similarly, Charity Hackett in *Park Row* is equated with the same world as Grant, she speaks French, and she is represented as a dangerously attractive vision. She appears to Mitchell one night as though she were a vision of purity, dressed in white fur with a sparkling diamond tiara. She is Mephistopheles, but in the guise of the good fairy, tempting Mitchell with wealth, comfort and success on the world's terms. Fuller makes clear the power of the appeal, the attractions of a well-furnished ivory tower; the measure of Mitchell's strength and courage is that he wants to succumb but doesn't. He remains an outsider fighting for his own vision of the truth, identifying with the bars, not the salons.

But it is nothing new to hear people defending a free Press and praising the search for and defence of truth. They are among the liberal clichés of our time. What Fuller does in *Park Row*, as in all his other films, is enact his moral truth. He doesn't just mouth slogans or make shallow films with a message: he embeds his moral truths in the structure of his movie. Mitchell says to one of his journalists, 'Don't tell me about it, write it.' Fuller doesn't just say things, he shows them.

So *Park Row* follows Mitchell as he fights for the truth. He is played by Gene Evans, one of the archetypal Fuller actors, who also played leading roles in *The Steel Helmet*, *Fixed Bayonets*, *Hell and High Water* and *Shock Corridor*. He is certainly no ivory-tower intellectual, or what Fuller describes as a 'chicken-hearted liberal'. He's tough and rough. He clearly has the physical stamina for the fight and he certainly has a fight on his hands. It has often been remarked that all Fuller's films are war films: as he himself says in *Pierrot le Fou*: 'Film is like a battleground.' He has a Manichean view of

They fought man-to-man...loved man-to-woman...and made history together on the most famous newspaper street in the world!

she had blood in her veins... *he had ink ...and guts!*

Samuel Fuller's

PARK ROW

The street of rogues... reporters ...and romance!

Samuel Fuller's "PARK ROW"

The picture with the page one punch!

starring GENE EVANS · MARY WELCH

with BELA KOVACS and HERBERT HEYES · Written, Produced and Directed by SAMUEL FULLER · Released thru UNITED ARTISTS

18

the universe. Good and evil are having one hell of a scrap and Fuller is reporting straight from the front line. Here *Park Row* is the scene of a physical fight for a free Press and all that a free Press stands for.

Fuller has the ability of all great directors to turn important abstract ideas into striking concrete actions on the screen; nor, like his journalist hero, is he afraid of powerful simple ideas, what might be called headline shots. For instance, in one continuous shot Mitchell punches a criminal responsible for maiming a young boy on his staff right out of his office into the street, until he ends up in close-up banging the thug's head against the inscription on Ben Franklin's statue. This shot conveys very directly Mitchell's personal commitment and energy, but it also says clearly that traditions of freedom don't just survive by their own force, they have to be actively defended. You mustn't just talk about a free Press, you must make one, and that's not easy. It is a question of character. Davenport, the aged journalist from the old days, writes his own obituary, which he turns into a tribute to Mitchell. In it he writes 'the Press is good or evil according to the character of those who direct it'.

When Fuller praises the sort of newspaper he admires, he is also defining the sort of movie he is trying to make. 'As I see it 95 per cent of films are born of frustration; of self-despair, of poverty, of ambition, for survival, for money, for fattening bank accounts; that's what's behind 95 per cent of films. I think 5 per cent, maybe less, are made because a man has an idea, an idea which he must express.' In *Park Row* Charity Hackett and the *Star* represent that 95 per cent – they have the money, the power and the prestige, but they produce a dull, dishonest newspaper without ideas. Hackett is like a studio boss, ruthless and irresponsible: Wiley, her business manager, has no ideals. He will even maim and kill to stop the *Globe*. Wiley is the typical producer – as Charity points out he is her creature and that is why her editor Spiro despises him. Spiro is the director who has sold out. He admires

Globe versus *Star*: Gene Evans (Mitchell) and Mary Welch (Hackett) in *Park Row*

Mitchell but hasn't the guts to follow him. The *Star* has the best newsprint and the best ink; Mitchell has to scrounge wrapping paper to print the *Globe*.

Fuller's films have often been disregarded because they are, as he himself describes them, cheap programme-fillers. But, like Mitchell, he has ideas and he is not inhibited by false notions of taste. There is a *Star* editorial conference in which Hackett berates her staff for not having thought of putting a cartoon on the front page as the *Globe* has done. Spiro points out that she would never have countenanced such a thing on her respectable *Star*. She agrees. Fuller has had similar opposition from respectable film criticism. He is concerned above all with impact; he wants his films to shout out the truth as he sees it. If it is whispered it will be drowned by the loud voice of hypocrisy. In *Park Row* Mitchell has some special 120 point type cut for the first-ever banner headline in the history of journalism.

But Fuller's stress on the primacy of the idea does not mean that he despises his tools: he doesn't make cheap pictures just for the sake of it, but for the independence it gives. And these quickies are very sophisticated technically. He is a virtuoso of the long fluid take and the striking camera position. Although he makes pictures quickly there is nothing slapdash about them. The key moment of *Park Row* is a shot of which Fuller is rightly proud, a shot that puts him technically in the same league as Welles, Ophuls and Mizoguchi and other masters of the moving camera. Mitchell is in the bar when he hears that his people are being attacked; he rushes out into Park Row and runs past struggling people. He goes into the *Star* office and confronts Spiro with his irresponsibility. He then rushes out of there and further along the street to the *Globe* office where he hears of the maiming of the boy. In a single shot Fuller takes in the whole location of his movie. In all Fuller movies there is a crucial moment when the violence inherent in any battle, any conflict, bursts into the open. This is the moment when the protagonists are finally committed to physical involvement, a commitment that Fuller is constantly forcing upon his audience. In this shot Fuller does several things simultaneously: he involves all the members of Park Row society in this violence, the bar, the *Star*, the *Globe* and the street that joins them. It is no good being an innocent bystander; as a member of society you're involved and responsible. He directly involves the audience in the headlong rush of Mitchell's flight, tying together the bar and the people, the *Globe* and good crusading journalism. It is because Mitchell in his person acts as the link and the *Star* stands physically between them, that the fight is important.

In conversation Fuller looks forward excitedly to technical developments in movie-making, for he sees it as a great but as yet unexploited means of education for propagating truth. His views about this are very close to Rossellini's, another exponent of the long take. He wants to dramatize history, to make films about Balzac and Beethoven, to show what great

Master of the moving camera: Fuller at work on *Run of the Arrow* and (opposite) *Fixed Bayonets*

guys they were. But above all he is always looking for a smaller, lighter, more flexible camera so that it can go anywhere, so that technique doesn't hamper the free flow of ideas. So *Park Row* is a film not only about Pulitzer but also about Mergenthaler, the inventor of linotype. Such technical innovations can bring creative freedom as long as they are in the right hands and are not used as just another way of making money. Hackett tries to buy Mergenthaler's invention, but he won't sell. He is committed to the ideal of good journalism, and, as Davenport says to Hackett, 'The joy of working for an ideal is the joy of living'. Sadly, in movie-making, the technique is so often in the service of money, which is hostile to ideas. So much of recent big budget film-making, even in the hands of really talented directors, shows this. As Fuller said to an interviewer: 'If I gave you five or eight million dollars, six stars and a great subject, you'd make a great film, but you

wouldn't have done anything. I couldn't detect what you yourself had contributed.'

One of the great problems in writing movie criticism is the impossibility of quoting. Because it is so difficult to convey the total effect of even one shot in a movie, let alone a sequence or a whole movie, the thematic elements that can be extracted and the meanings contained in the dialogue will always tend to be stressed at the expense of the overall effect. Many of the differences in approach to the American cinema between the French and the Anglo-Saxon schools of critics can be attributed to the fact that many French critics have a less than total grasp of the English language. This leads to strengths and weaknesses on both sides. The French critic will tend to misjudge individual movies because of his inability to assess the tone of many scenes. So much meaning can attach to the way a line is said. But free from a slavish adherence to the

obvious linguistic meanings he is often better able to see the thematic unity in a director's work, especially that embodied in *mise-en-scéne*, all those attributes of the cinema which are not in the script. The Anglo-Saxon critic, especially as he will usually come to movies with a primarily literary cultural background, will tend to base his judgement over-heavily on the script and also to be put off by comparatively superficial breaks in tonal felicity. A false delivery of one line can often throw an Anglo-Saxon critic off his balance for a whole sequence and build up a subconscious distrust of the movie that can never be assuaged.

As far as American critics are concerned, there is a further cause of blockage where their own cinema is concerned: this coalesces round the issue of superficial realism. We accept, I think, that the central tradition of cinema is realist, that the recording of what is in front of the camera has an important role to play. But we should not make of this an exclusive requirement. One of the great qualities of the movies is their heterogeneous inclusive nature, the fact that they explore in valid ways the whole range from the most extreme artifice in animation to the extremes of documentary realism. I find both extremes in this range unsatisfactory but I would be unwilling to incorporate these personal dislikes into any sort of critical dogma. I just stay away from the movies. However, because realism is so important, if only because identification is such a key weapon in the movie-maker's armoury, superficial failures to satisfy an audience's realistic desires can result in a neglect of the essential meaning and impact of a film. Talking to Americans about American movies one continually comes up against this difficulty: they will dismiss a film because they don't feel the sociological background is right. 'People don't talk, dress, act like that' is levelled as a dismissive accusation.

What relevance has all this to a critique of Fuller? He has, I think, been misjudged by British and above all American critics because he does not satisfy, nor does he intend to satisfy, the superficial desire for realism. He uses dialogue as a

25

The B-feature look: Warren Hsieh and Gene Barry in *China Gate* means of delivering slogans rather than as an aspect of behaviour, or as part of the detailed build-up of a character in the way that, for instance, Nicholas Ray uses dialogue. The acting style he favours is similarly broad. Why he does this I will examine in a moment. As for his settings, because he has in general made what he calls programme pictures, B-features, he has worked fast and cheap and with one or two exceptions his pictures lack those production values that give to empty exercises by less talented directors a gloss of realism. This particularly applies to movies like *China Gate*, *Hell and High Water* and *Verboten*. It is indicative of his talents that he has developed a style to exploit these deficiencies, and in recent movies such as *Shock Corridor* and *The Naked Kiss* his style has become beautifully bare and ascetic, stripped to the essentials as in the late movies of Fritz Lang. But production values can count. *Merrill's Marauders* is Fuller's best war movie partly because it is his most expensive.

Just as the essence of Fuller's themes is conflict and contradiction, so too is the essence of his style. For its basic ingredients, high-impact dynamic montage and long takes, are normally antithetical. Fuller's style conveys not grace but energy. His movies are as brutal and harsh to look at and to hear as the world they depict. We are far here from the soft misty felicities of what is the current trendy cinema style, a product of Eastmancolor and long-focus lenses, as seen in *The Graduate* or *Elvira Madigan*. Those movies encourage their audience to lie back and drift off into a dream world. Fuller's movies come down off the screen and shake you by the neck. As one of the soldiers says in *Merrill's Marauders*: 'When this is all over I'm going to line my children up against a wall and tell them what it was like here in Burma. If they don't cry I'll beat the hell out of them.' These two aims are not normally combined in the work of one director. There are directors who tell what it was like here and there are directors who beat the hell out of them: the former, a dominant tradition in the cinema, are impressionistic directors, the latter expressionistic.

Only Fuller and Welles manage to hold a balance between these two styles.

The impressionistic school is associated stylistically with the functional camera and its logical development, the long take, together presenting an objective view of the world. The masters of this school, Hawks, Ford, Renoir, Ophuls, Mizoguchi and Rossellini all have notable stylistic differences, but their cinema is based upon freedom of individual action. The life they reveal pre-exists its existence on the screen and is therefore outside the total control of the director. Their cameras sit and watch, or follow and track, their characters as these characters work out their destiny. It is not that we are unaware of the camera, but the characters are always superior to it. Rossellini's long takes express his camera's (and therefore his) patient humility before the free will of his characters. They also express God's eternal watchfulness and a Franciscan acceptance of life in all its diverse rhythms. Renoir's fluid camera serves a similar purpose but from a humanist rather than a religious point of view. Ophuls's movies would appear to be a denial of this connection between freedom and the long take, for they reveal his characters as puppets ruled by an implacable fate. Ophuls's fatalism, however, is embodied not in his long takes but in his flashback structure. The power of his movies comes in large part from the tension between this retrospective fatalism and the powerful illusion of freedom conveyed by the long takes. Indeed, at the end of *Lola Montès*, the ring-master who represents the director is in love not with the circus puppet he has helped to create but with the trapped, suffering woman hidden within this puppet and outside his control.

The ultimate development of this style can be seen in Preminger, and it is no accident that Fuller admires Preminger. Fuller is one of the virtuosi of the long take; according to Luc Moullet, *Verboten* contains less than a hundred shots, including one of five minutes forty-seven seconds, one of five minutes twenty-nine seconds and one of three minutes twenty-nine seconds. Fuller himself claims that the scene with Moe Williams at the police station in *Pickup on South Street* does in fact last ten minutes and has thirty-two different camera positions, although in the edited film this take is broken up by one cutaway shot of the FBI man. These long takes are clearly an important ingredient in Fuller's love of the cinema. They are an expression of his restless energy. He described recently to a group of which I was a member a forty-minute shot that he plans for his next movie. The sequence follows an American patrol being pursued through the jungle by the Vietcong. The track will stretch the distance it takes that patrol to go in forty minutes, and Fuller will then use two cameras and overlap them at the beginning and end of each ten-minute magazine, changing from one to the other just as you change from one projector to another in the cinema, and, as he put it, 'I'll tell the actors they must just keep going, whatever happens they must keep up with us, I'm not waiting for them.'

These long takes are especially remarkable in a director who has in general made quick, cheap B-features. As can be seen in TV films, the conditions of this type of movie-making usually rule out any elaboration of technique. Scenes are in general reduced to a quick establishing shot and then into static close-ups for the dialogue, so as to cut lighting and camera movements to a minimum, thus saving time and money but above all risk. But it is this very risk element that Fuller enjoys, for these long takes are not just the response to a technical challenge, nor are they there just to give that feeling of visual richness which is present in even the cheapest of Fuller's pictures. They embody certain of his thematic preoccupations. A long take becomes a microcosm of Fuller's world and the actor becomes the existential hero. He has freedom of action, he is setting out on a journey in which every movement and every word risks all. That is to say, if he fluffs they must start again, and as the take goes on the tension rises as there is more and more to lose. Fuller has himself described with glee the

The actors confined by the set: the cave in *Fixed Bayonets*

sweat his actors and his crew get into as these takes progress, with the whole enterprise likely to blow up in their faces at any moment. As he puts it, 'long takes irritate the crew and irritate the actors'.

But it is also noticeable that these takes are often confined in very restricted locations, made more restricted by the avoidance of wide-angle lenses. The newspaper office in *Park Row*, the police station in *Pickup on South Street*, the office of the American military government in *Verboten*, the cave in *Fixed Bayonets*; and even out of doors as in *Merrill's Marauders* the shot is restricted by vegetation, water and rocks. This produces a three-way tension between the actors, the camera and the props. We feel the actor physically assailed on all sides. The set becomes for him and for the camera like the maze at Shadzup for the troops in *Merrill's Marauders*.

29

Violent cross-cutting between a murder investigation and love-scene: James Shigeta (Joe) and Victoria Shaw (Christine) in *The Crimson Kimono*

At the Edinburgh Film Festival in 1969, Fuller recounted how, after rehearsing a scene, he changes the props around to disconcert the actors. Like his characters they can never be sure exactly what's happening. So these takes combine a feeling of extreme freedom with extreme frustration, the typical Fuller mixture.

Just as the Fuller hero bursts out of this situation through violence, Fuller breaks the rhythm in his long takes by violently dynamic montage. His cuts are often the formal equivalent of Tolly's clenched fist or Kelly's swinging handbag. They operate on the audience much like the rhythm of war as shown in *Fixed Bayonets*, where the Lieutenant's call to take a break is immediately followed by a violent enemy bombardment; where, as Rock says, relax for an instant and they will knife you in the back. One thinks of the huge close-up of Brent's eye in *Verboten*, preceding a slow pan round the room to take in his rifle, Helga, a portrait of Adolf Hitler, and Brent lying on the bed; the violent cross-cutting between the love scenes and the murder investigation scenes in *The Crimson Kimono*; the superimposition of the titles 'Grant killed by prostitute' over shots of the inhabitants of Grantville reading about the murder in *The Naked Kiss*; the close-up of the trigger finger at Denno's moment of personal decision in *Fixed Bayonets*. The whole forward movement of *Underworld USA* is based on a series of such shock transitions, no scene held a second beyond its culminating moment.

More often than not those shocks are achieved not by editing but by camera movements within the long takes, so adding to the feeling of disorientation and chaos by forcing two disparate formal manœuvres together, combining the long take and montage in one shot. For instance, the scene in which the GIs rub each other's feet in *Fixed Bayonets* and which ends by tracking into close-up of Rock's stamping feet; or the scene in which Brent first meets Helga in *Verboten*, ending on a close-up of his hand lying on a copy of *Mein Kampf*; or the opening shot of *Run of the Arrow*, a track in close-up over

Run of the Arrow: lining up a shot; Rod Steiger (O'Meara) jubilant over the body of Ralph Meeker (Lt. Driscoll)

the debris of war that pulls back to reveal the Union cavalry-
man slumped on his horse as he picks his way slowly over the
battlefield. He is shot and falls unconscious at our feet.

But Fuller never dwells on his effects, he never allows his
shots to slow up the action of the film. And this is part of a
general strategy. Just as his characters can never rest on their
laurels, nor can his movie. Death, for instance, is never dwelt
on; even a beautifully powerful image like the wedding veil
over Grant's dead face is held only for an instant. Life is
pushing the movie along. When Silent Tongue is saved from
the quicksand in *Run of the Arrow*, we cut away immediately
the trooper falls in. The fact, having had its effect on the
audience, is never mentioned again. In *Fixed Bayonets*,
once people are dead the camera leaves them instantly to
concentrate on the actions of the living.

This tension between life and death, beauty and ugliness,
is often sandwiched into one shot. Fuller excels at single
images of a powerful but complex significance that embody
the basic tensions of his world. Mount Fujiyama framed
by the boots of the dead sergeant in *House of Bamboo* – it
manages to be both a beautiful and a horribly crude image,
to contain and hold in balance both the natural beauty of the
world and the horrors perpetrated in this setting. The image
of Griff shot in his bath has the same effect, both beautiful
and horrible at the same time. Buff lying in bed in *The Naked
Kiss*, cradling a photo of her father in uniform who was killed
in Korea, is a typical Fuller image. It forces into the same
frame sensuous young womanhood at its most tender, and
death in war, both the possibilities and impossibilities of life,
hope and its denial. Moreover, the two visions are linked, for
Buff is asking her father to forgive her for lying. Her father
died to protect a society in which Buff wanted to be a prostitute
rather than a nurse, and which is so sunk in hypocrisy that she
will lie rather than help the woman who stopped her becoming
a prostitute. Such images abound in Fuller movies: Short
Round wearing an American Army uniform, his face smeared

with chocolate; the wounded village girl clinging to Stock's neck in *Merrill's Marauders*.

These images are in the expressionistic tradition. So also is Fuller's shock-editing style. The expressionistic director, Hitchcock for instance or Lang, assaults the audience. He manipulates images to create a world that only exists on the screen. He points the camera not so much at the world as at the audience. It is camera-gun rather than camera-eye. 'You can't show war as it really is on the screen, with all the blood and gore. Perhaps it would be better if you could fire real shots over the audience's head every night, you know, and have actual casualties in the theatre.' The expressionist director wishes to manipulate the audience just as he manipulates his images, and deny it freedom of either choice or action. He says, not 'Look, this is how it is', but 'Look, this is how I feel.' As Fuller puts it, 'It is not necessary for the camera to move or for the characters to move. What matters is that the emotion of the audience should move. I call that the emotion picture.'

It is again no accident that Fuller is a friend and admirer of Fritz Lang, for like Lang's films, Fuller's are social indictments. They are not meant to be contemplated; they are like newspaper exposés of which the purpose is to inspire corrective action. Both Lang and Fuller use the format of the newspaper in their movies: signs, photographs, often newspapers themselves. One thinks of Tolly's prison record, Vic Farrar's temperature chart, and the recurrent newspaper headlines in *Underworld USA* – 'Connors Defies Uncle Sam.' Sandy's briefing of his gang in *House of Bamboo*, and the scenes in the office of the American military government in *Verboten* with their maps and photographs, have a particular Langian flavour, although Lang would have cut Fuller's long takes into a series of more static self-contained shots. The resemblances between *Underworld USA* and *The Big Heat* I will examine in more detail later.

This desire to come directly to grips with contemporary reality leads Fuller into an increasing use of documentary or

34

Use of newspaper format: *Verboten*

pseudo-documentary. At the beginning of *China Gate* he sets the political and military context of his film with documentary footage. *House of Bamboo* starts with a factual statement: 'This film was photographed in Tokyo, Yokohama and the Japanese countryside; the year is 1954.' *The Crimson Kimono* opens again with the exact location and time superimposed over actuality shots of Los Angeles streets. *Merrill's Marauders* starts with a short historical lecture backed up by maps. In *Verboten* the key action is motivated by newsreels of the Nuremberg Tribunal and of Nazi atrocities. *The Naked Kiss* is given a precise contemporary date in the mid sixties.

As with Lang, much of the power and distinction of Fuller's movies comes from a feeling of the director's unease with the medium itself. Just as he breaks out of his long takes with montage and out of fictional situations with documentary

35

presentation, there is a sense in which Fuller is forced to destroy his medium as he creates, just as Brecht was forced to destroy the traditional theatre and for similar reasons. This is one of the reasons, I think, for the critical neglect of Fuller: he assaults the preconceptions of film critics just as he assaults the social preconceptions of his audience. There is an urgency and increasing desperation in his films which sits uneasily within the limits of normal narrative, Hollywood-produced cinema and which has forced him, as it forced Lang, to examine the very basis of his art. The cinema is an art of appearances, but in the Fuller world appearances are a trap. They hide reality more than they reveal it. Just as Lang in *Beyond A Reasonable Doubt* involves the audience in the fake nature of documentary screen reality, so in *The Crimson Kimono* Fuller examines the essential ambiguity of the screen image in a movie which completely destroys the limits of the crime genre. The impressionist tradition has used the human face as a vehicle for conveying thoughts and feelings; Fuller uses the cliché of Oriental inscrutability to destroy this possibility. The face becomes a mask, the screen becomes a mirror reflecting back the preconceptions of the audience. As Chris says to Joe, 'You saw what you wanted to see.' So whatever a director puts up there on the screen, the audiences will remain trapped in their own manifold individualities: their reaction will be entirely subjective, their and the director's preoccupations mutually irrelevant.

But this will be so only as long as we don't think about what is happening on the screen; as long as we identify completely with the action of the movie our reaction will be entirely subjective. But if our viewpoint can be constantly changed we might be led to question that subjective reaction. Brecht's description of what he was trying to do with the theatre (quoted by Raymond Williams in *Modern Tragedy*) applies to Fuller's movies. 'It is a sort of summary of what the spectator wishes to see of life. Since, however, he sees at the same time certain things that he does not wish to see, and thus sees his

Documentary realism: shooting *The Crimson Kimono* in the streets of Los Angeles

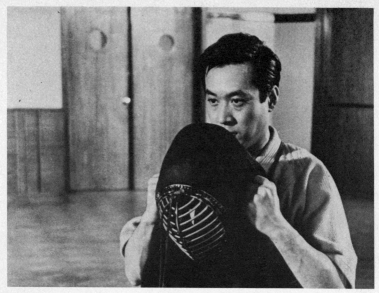

The face as mask: James Shigeta in *The Crimson Kimono*

wishes not only fulfilled but criticized . . . complex seeing must be practised. . . . Thinking *above* the flow of the play is more important than thinking from *within* the flow of the play.'

There are many other echoes of Brecht in Fuller's work: a similar liking for gangsters and prostitutes; the use of outsiders to obtain a critical viewpoint of conventional society and express disgust with conventional moral values, a similar lapse, at times, into a too easy cynicism; a similar comparison between gangsterism and Fascism (compare *Arturo Ui* with *Underworld USA* and *Verboten*). There is the cultivation of a similar broad acting style and broad, almost vulgar, compositions. Both Brecht and Fuller are using a cartoon effect, and Fuller's stress in *Park Row* on the use of front-page cartoons in newspapers is significant.

So the audience of a Fuller movie, like a Fuller hero, is faced by a constantly shifting interplay of differing realities; a

Fuller movie is like those 3-D photographs produced by superimposing two views of the same scene from different angles. This technique is carried to its extremes in *China Gate* and *Verboten*, where themes of the widest general political significance are superimposed upon a highly personal human relationship. I feel that in both cases the attempt fails, and breaks the medium wide open in the process. This may be because both films suffer from being made cheaply; it is the technique of *War and Peace*, and maybe this cannot be done on a small scale. None the less it is probably the most fruitful development in modern cinema and a direction Fuller continues to explore. For what Fuller is attempting in all his movies is the solution to what Raymond Williams in *Modern Tragedy* has rightly diagnosed as the central dilemma of modern tragedy, the split between the personal and the social: '. . . the three characteristically new systems of thinking, in our own time – Marxism, Freudianism, Existentialism – are all, in their most common forms, tragic. Man can achieve his full life only after violent conflict; man is essentially frustrated, and divided against himself, while he lives in society; man is torn by intolerable contradictions, in a condition of essential absurdity'. Fuller's importance lies not only in the fact of his daring to handle all three of these basic themes, but in his method of so doing.

All modern dramatists and film-makers have been forced to reject either the personal or the social view of man's tragic condition. The objective school, Preminger in *Advise and Consent* for instance, while allowing the audience to make up its own mind also allows it the dangerous luxury of avoiding any emotional commitment. The intellectual recognition of moral relativism can so easily become an amoral nihilism, a shrug of the shoulders. In this context the long silence of Nicholas Ray is, I am afraid, tragically relevant. But the subjective approach, on the other hand, can so easily become propaganda, an emotional response at the expense of thought, or what is less serious but more disturbingly prevalent – cheap escapism. We find this at its most distinguished in John Ford, at its silliest in *The Graduate* or *Easy Rider*. In England the critics of the *Sequence* school took John Ford as their master. He is a great film-maker but a dangerous example, and those recent hits, *Morgan* and *If . . .*, both distressingly share the weaknesses of the subjective approach without the Fordian distinction.

In *Verboten* Fuller combines the objective and subjective approaches. Franz lives the subjective view of Germany and gains an objective view by going to the trials at Nuremberg and seeing the newsreels. Brent's development is in the opposite direction. He starts as an objective outsider and is drawn ever deeper into emotional subjective involvement. He starts as an invading foreign soldier and ends as a German civilian.

But the difficulty of maintaining the unique but difficult balance between these two traps is evident in Fuller's work. In *Park Row* and in *Verboten* journalism and the cinema are seen as the great educating media; leaders of the fight against those screens of hypocrisy that bar the way of the Fuller hero towards self-fulfilment and a healthy society of equal individuals. But in Fuller's movies we see the lie gaining strength: in *Shock Corridor* the journalist is corrupt and goes mad trying to find the truth. In *The Naked Kiss* the cinema too is indicted. It is crucially significant that Kelly succumbs to the illusion of marriage to Grant against the evidence of her senses (i.e. 'the naked kiss' that reveals his perversion to her) under the influence of Grant's home movies. Now a documentary on Venice, shot by Fuller himself, has become part of the fatal illusion, another weapon in the hands of the hypocrites and corrupters. This is allied to a general disillusionment, not so much with art itself as with the uses to which it is put. Beethoven's music is tightly linked to the movie shots of Venice. Fuller's known love of Beethoven is a measure of the desperate nature of his analysis of the movie medium in *The Naked Kiss*.

Kelly quotes Goethe: 'Nothing is worse than active ignorance.' The terrifying growth of the big lie in American society and especially politics, is attested to by countless American writers and intellectuals. 'Politics was the place where finally nobody meant what they said' (Norman Mailer). Noam Chomsky in his book *American Power and the New Mandarins* includes the whole American intellectual establishment in Mailer's indictment. The heroism of Fuller's continuing achievement is his fight against the growing powers of the lie with a medium that he knows is being corrupted from within by its very nature. Fuller is central because his way seems the best way if the cinema is to retain a position of cultural importance. If his struggle fails maybe the cinema is doomed to fiddle while the world burns.

2 : Fuller and the Individual

'The masterless.

  '"Ca ca Caliban,

  Get a new master, be a new man."

  'What did the Pilgrim Fathers come for then when they came so gruesomely over the black sea? Oh, it was in a black spirit. A black revulsion from Europe, from the old authority of Europe, from kings and bishops and popes. And more. When you look into it, more. They were black masterful men, they wanted something else. No kings, no bishops maybe. Even no God Almighty. But also, no more of this new "humanity" which followed the Renaissance. None of this new liberty which was to be so pretty in Europe. Something grimmer, by no means free and easy.

  'America has never been easy, and is not easy today. Americans have always been at a certain tension. Their liberty is a thing of sheer will, sheer tension. . . .'
D. H. Lawrence, *Studies in Classic American Literature*.

Fuller's movies are studies of that liberty which is sheer will, sheer tension. His movies examine what is in philosophy and art the central problem of our time, the crisis of individualism. Here it is important to stress his Americanism as evidence of his centrality. Of course individualism has been a central problem in modern European art too, but it is I think significant that those writers such as Camus and Malraux, who have made it their especial concern, have used frontier situations as the settings for their examinations: Algiers, Indo-China and China. The interest, particularly in France, in American art, movies and jazz, stems from a realization that the crisis of individualism is an essentially American problem. As D. H. Lawrence pointed out, the United States was set up by disaffected Europeans as a testing-ground for new ways of life. It was very specifically to be a home for individual liberty in a way no other society had been, and in a way that to this day no other society has been. Fuller's movies are reports on how this experiment is going by an insider, by someone who, as an American, is living this experiment himself. They are not the reports of a coolly objective outside observer. They are full of directly felt pain and exhilaration.

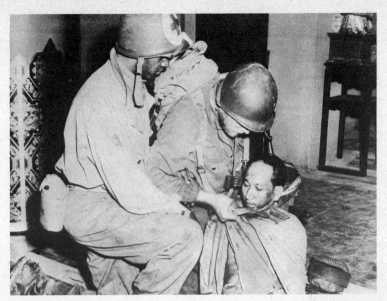

'If you die I'll kill you'. Gene Evans (Sgt. Zack) with the North Korean Major in *The Steel Helmet*

So the Fuller hero, or rather protagonist, for he or she is portrayed in resolutely unheroic terms, is the pure American, absolute individualism. Fuller's cinema is a cinema of contradictions because a fundamental contradiction lies at the heart of pure individualism. As Peter Wollen puts it in his study of Boetticher: 'For individualism death is an absolute limit which cannot be transcended; it renders the life which precedes it absurd. How then can there be any meaningful individual action during life? How can individual action have any value if it cannot have transcendent value, because of the absolutely devaluing limit of death?' This contradiction is constantly underlined in Fuller's movies: Sergeant Zack in *The Steel Helmet* grabs the North Korean Major he has just shot and shouts, 'If you die, I'll kill you.' Moe in *Pickup on South Street* is saving for a fancy burial: 'If I was buried in Potter's Field it would just about kill me.' When Skip collects

43

Framed by death: John Ireland (Bob Ford) and Barbara Britton (Cynthy) in *I Shot Jesse James*; and the death of Tolly's father in *Underworld USA*

her coffin from the barge taking it to Potter's Field he is asked what he is going to do with it: 'Bury it.' A mercenary in *China Gate* says, 'This is the life for me, but I have to die to live it.'

In a Fuller movie we are rarely allowed to forget the presence of death, most obviously by his characters being placed in a war situation where the threat of death is constant. But the movies are also often framed by deaths. *I Shot Jesse James* opens with the shooting of the bank cashier, is followed by the shooting of Jesse James, and ends with the death of Bob Ford. *Run of the Arrow*, by a brilliant irony, begins and ends with the double death of one man: in the opening shot of the movie Driscoll is shot by O'Meara, and near the end he is shot again by the same man and with the same bullet. We find this circular motion also in *The Crimson Kimono*, which opens with the stripper Sugar Torch being murdered as she runs down the street and ends with her murderer being shot as she too attempts to escape in the street. *Underworld USA* opens with the death of Devlin Sr and ends with the death of Devlin Jr in almost identical garbage-strewn alleys, and just as Tolly threw himself upon his father's dead upturned face crying 'Dad!', so Cuddles throws herself upon Tolly's upturned face crying 'Tolly!' The absurdity is underlined when Sandy tells Cuddles she must sing on Smith or 'Tolly died for nothing.' The unavoidable nature of his death is stressed by the circular motion, but also by the scene in the park where Cuddles tells Tolly that the only way they will come out of this is on a marble slab, which, of course, goes for everybody.

The absolute limit of death is also stressed stylistically. Fuller never holds a scene, especially a death scene. 'Don't stop the fight when someone is shot – if a guy is killed, carry on, what else can you do?' So death is treated completely unsentimentally. In *Fixed Bayonets* a Chinese jeep-driver is shot, and one of the patrol triumphantly discovers dry socks on the body. But the bodies of one's own side are treated as unceremoniously. 'Strip him of everything we can use, wrap him in a blanket, bury him, mark him', runs through the

Verboten: James Best (Brent) uses the body of his dead companion for a screen

movie like a refrain. In *Verboten*, Brent immediately strips the cartridge-belt from his dead companion and uses his body for a screen. There is neither the hymn-singing round the grave as in Ford, nor the cataloguing of meagre personal possessions, as in Hawks. Death is just the end. In *Park Row* Davenport explains to the young printer's devil the use of a journalists' 30 at the end of a story, and says, 'The end of a story is when there is no more to say.' In Fuller's movies death is 30; it is the end of a sequence or the end of a movie.

It is this stylistic strategy and the attitude it embodies that explain the total absence of sadism in Fuller's movies, for all their violence. One can imagine what some directors would have made, in the present lip-smacking atmosphere, of the deaths in *Underworld USA*. Fuller's work is completely free

The end of a sequence: the death of the cavalry trooper in *Run of the Arrow*

of that pornography of violence one finds, for instance, in such recently admired movies as *Point Blank* and *The Wild Bunch*. The position of the audience *vis-à-vis The Wild Bunch* is exactly comparable with the children who watch the ants killing the scorpion: in Fuller movies, human beings, like ants or scorpions, are just swiftly stamped on. It is significant that Fuller, though he shares some of Hemingway's preoccupations and is a close friend of Boetticher (his own 16-mm footage was used as trailer material for *The Bullfighter and the Lady*), finds bullfighting ludicrous.

The problems of individualism are exposed in Fuller's movies by stressing the loner nature of his protagonists. They are all outsiders cut off from conventional civilized society. The perfect objective correlative of their situation is the high-

47

angle shot in *Pickup on South Street* of the shack in which Skip lives, a small wooden box surrounded by water, jutting out and away from the very edge of human society, the city, connected by a narrow gangplank. These outsiders face the absurd by living a lie in the name of truth; they are apparently utterly cynical realists, outsiders by choice; but O'Meara's 'I'm a rebel because I choose to be' is, as we are aware, deeply ironic. For these hard-bitten cynics in fact act not out of choice but from a deep inner compulsion. One of the dialectics upon which Fuller's work is based is that between the apparent and the real reason for his characters' actions. The motto of *Hell and High Water* is: every man has a reason for living and a price for dying. In *House of Bamboo* Mariko asks Spanier how much money he is being paid to run the risks he does as a double agent. 'Sergeant's pay,' he replies, '190 dollars and 30 cents a month.' The gap between the dangers run and the financial reward makes the implausibility of that as a motive brutally clear, nor is there any hint that Spanier is doing the job out of loyalty to the Army or to the United States.

Fuller's protagonists often present rational practical reasons for their actions, their price for dying, but Fuller never allows us to forget their reason for living. Joe, in *The Crimson Kimono*, says he is a policeman because the job is steady and there is a pension. But in fact he does it because police work gives him protection from his own racial confusions, provides him with a role in which he can escape from the true imperatives of the self. Bob Ford kills Jesse James not for the reward, which by the time he gets it is laughably small, but because he loves Cynthy. Indeed, he immediately turns the reward into a diamond engagement-ring, a symbol of his love for Cynthy. Reavis contemptuously turns down whatever huge sum the US Government offers him to give up his claim to Arizona: he wants to be baron of Arizona and devotes his whole life to that end. Sergeant Zack's apparent aim is personal survival: 'I want to come through this', but he

48

Their reason for living: Vincent Price (Reavis) in *The Baron of Arizona*; Thelma Ritter (Moe) with Jean Peters (Candy) in *Pickup on South Street*

agrees to lead the patrol through no man's land for a box of stogies and he can only realize his personality in terms of war. He is pure soldier. Fuller is interested in people who volunteer for war: the mercenaries of *China Gate* and *Hell and High Water*, the Second World War retreads* of *The Steel Helmet* and *Fixed Bayonets*, the volunteers of *Merrill's Marauders*. Such men heighten the absurd contradiction between life and death. In a long dialogue scene in *Fixed Bayonets* Denno quizzes Rock (played, like Zack, by Gene Evans, and essentially the same character) as to why he stays in the Army. It becomes clear that he cannot explain it in rational terms; it is just the way he is.

The general atmosphere of *Pickup on South Street* is one of mercenary cynicism. When Skip learns where Candy got his address he says, 'Moe's all right, she's got to eat.' As Moe herself puts it: 'Some people peddle apples, lumber, lamb chops, I peddle information.' But in fact she is not doing it to eat but in order to save for a fancy burial. She refuses to give Skip's address to the Communist agent, but not because of an instinctive healthy anti-Communism as some critics would have us believe. As she admits: 'What do I know about Commies? Nothing.' She refuses to give the information firstly out of loyalty to Skip, and secondly because she is tired and just wants to die. Candy starts by being prepared to make love to Skip in order to get the microfilm off him and ends, out of love for Skip, by co-operating with the police at great risk to herself. Skip starts by playing both ends against the middle to obtain the highest possible bid for the microfilm, and ends by beating up the Communist agent because he had beaten up Candy.

The mercenaries in *China Gate* and *Hell and High Water* are fighting on a contract for money, but in support of an idealistic cause, the crusade against Communism. This basic paradox is illustrated on a personal level. Brock is not fighting for the money or the cause. As Lucky Legs points out: 'You came here to fight for a Chinese baby.' He is trying to blot out

* Veterans who signed on again for the Korean war.

The mercenary in the service of the ideal: Gene Barry (Brock) blows up the bomb-dump in *China Gate*

the vision of his own son, who looks Chinese. He is fighting because he couldn't face facts that involved people. Goldie is fighting out of a rabid anti-Communism: 'I have come to finish something we didn't finish in Korea. There are still a lot of live Commies.' The irrationality of this motivation is stressed by cutting straight to the nightmare vision of the Russian soldier. Tolly Devlin, the most cynical and ruthless of all Fuller's individualistic protagonists, is motivated first by personal revenge at any risk to himself and finally goes to his death because of love for Cuddles.

Being an outsider is accepted as a fact of existence. When Candy asks Skip how he became a pickpocket, he rounds on her with: 'How did you become a pickpocket? How did you become what you are? Things happen, that's how.' The inescapability of this destiny is stressed by linking it to the highly personal nature of the characters' choices of action.

Lucky Legs is a prostitute who agrees to lead an expedition against her Vietminh lover, not for a bar in Saigon, but so that her son can go to the United States. Kelly, another prostitute, in *The Naked Kiss*, takes only what's owing to her when she knocks out her pimp and then follows the small-town circuit as a lone operator. She gives up prostitution, not for moral reasons, but because she sees lines on her face. Fuller's cinema is a cinema of confusion. Confusion between the cynical, mercenary surface and the deep irrational drives of his characters is only one of many such confusions.

America is a country based on freedom, a country of masterless men. As Fuller says, 'Without liberty life wouldn't be worth living.' But it is also a country based on the historical fact of slavery. Fuller is one of the great American directors because he has examined more deeply and consistently than any other director the confusions and tensions that such a contradiction places at the heart of the American religion of individualism. The Fuller protagonist is the White Negro of Norman Mailer's *Advertisements for Myself*: 'If the fate of twentieth-century man is to live with death from adolescence to premature senescence, why then, the only life-giving answer is to accept the terms of death, to live with death as immediate danger, to divorce oneself from society, to exist without roots, to set out on that uncharted journey into the rebellious imperatives of the self. In short, whether the life is criminal or not, the decision is to encourage the psychopath in oneself, to explore that domain of experience where security is boredom and therefore sickness, and one exists in the present, in that enormous present which is without past or future, memory or planned intention, the life where a man must go on until he is beat, where he must gamble with his energies through all those small or large crises of courage and unforeseen situations which beset his day.' Fuller's movies give concrete expression to 'that uncharted journey into the rebellious imperatives of the self'. His protagonists are involved in journeys or quests. Sergeant Kenner in *House of*

The uncharted journey: *Merrill's Marauders*

Bamboo is searching for the man who killed the US Army sergeant; Charlie and Joe in *The Crimson Kimono* are tracking down a murderer; Lucky Legs and her band of foreign mercenaries in *China Gate* track through the jungle in search of the Communist ammunition-dump; Adam Jones and his mercenary crew in their submarine in *Hell and High Water* search for a secret atom plant; O'Meara in *Run of the Arrow* goes off in search of a new country and a new nationality; Merrill's marauders spend the whole movie on a trek through enemy-occupied jungle and swamp; Tolly Devlin pursues his father's killers; Johnny Barrett in *Shock Corridor* enters a mental hospital and goes down the long corridor in search of a murderer; Kelly begins and ends *The Naked Kiss* like Odysseus on an endless journey from town to town.

These searches undertaken by Fuller's characters are, like the motives for which they are undertaken, deeply ambiguous.

A trip into himself: Peter Breck (Johnny Barrett) in *Shock Corridor*

Their goal is not what it seems to be. Lucky Legs, apparently leading an expedition to destroy the Communist ammunition-dump, is in fact searching for the truth of her own split nature: is it her Communist lover or an American future for her son that she wants most? For her there is no resolution except in suicide. O'Meara, at the end of his journey, is back where he started, confronting and shooting Driscoll, fulfilling an obscure ritualistic process of revenge. Tolly Devlin, too, ends where he had begun. The movie opens with him kneeling over a body beneath a blood donation poster in a garbage-strewn alley. The movie ends in the same situation, but now his is the body. While apparently pursuing his father's killers, he was really seeking his own death. In *The Crimson Kimono* it is not the solution of the murder that is important but, as Charlie puts it, the busting of Joe's own case, the solution of his racial and cultural dilemmas. Johnny

Barrett's trip into the mental hospital in search of a murderer is in fact a trip into himself and the discovery of his own insanity. Kelly's search for goodness becomes a revelation of evil.

These contradictions are further compounded by the atmosphere of treachery in which the protagonists find themselves. All Fuller's characters become double agents or renegades, acting out a complex dialectic of loyalty and treachery. Sergeant Kenner in *House of Bamboo* is a double agent with a girl friend who is not really his girl friend. Just as he betrays Sandy he is in turn betrayed to Sandy by the journalist double agent who has infiltrated police headquarters. Bob Ford in *I Shot Jesse James* shoots his best friend in the back; Reavis's whole life is devoted to forging a claim to the State of Arizona, and in order to do that he must pretend to be a monk and a gipsy and must turn a poor peasant girl into the last of an aristocratic line. Denno in *Fixed Bayonets* hides his cowardice, his inability to kill a man; O'Meara tries to turn himself into a Sioux; Barrett pretends to be mad; and Kelly hides her prostitute's past beneath a nurse's uniform. A continual irony underlies Fuller's examination of individualism. The search for and protection of oneself implies its own denial.

The world through which Fuller's protagonists move is not an attractive one. It is a violent world, producing in many spectators reactions of violent antipathy. Audiences in a moviehouse will always tend to identify with what is happening on the screen and Fuller uses this almost physical involvement as well as anyone. But this tendency to identification is both the strength and the weakness of movies, because the audience, to the extent that it sees itself up there on the screen, wants to be flattered. There is a scene in *Shock Corridor* in which the mad nuclear scientist is sketching Johnny Barrett; when he has finished he shows the sketch to Johnny who violently rejects it, refusing to accept it as a portrait of himself. This is a key stage in his breakdown, and

Reavis disguised as a monk in *The Baron of Arizona*; the mad nuclear scientist (Gene Evans) draws Barrett in *Shock Corridor*

similar to the reaction of many to Fuller's movies. Fuller doesn't flatter his audiences; he rubs our noses in our own dirt. This is particularly offensive to the liberal humanist school of criticism who still wish to believe that if all is not for the best in the best of all possible worlds, at least it soon will be. They wish to see movies in which the characters' finer feelings triumph, in which men and women are noble, honest, true, love each other and are kind to animals as well. They attack anyone who shows them a world which does not correspond to their rosy view, and they assume that the creators of such movies must share the vices and enjoy the horrors that they portray.

Fuller's view of the world is bleak. Mac says in *The Crimson Kimono*: 'Life is like a battle, somebody has to get a bloody nose.' As many critics have observed, Fuller is always making war movies. His world is close to Hobbes's: 'continual fear, and danger of violent death; and the life of man solitary, poor, nasty, brutish, and short'. It is easy for us in the comparatively settled, secure societies of Western Europe to dismiss both Fuller and Hobbes as embodying an absurdly limited view of human life. But we should remember that Hobbes developed his theories just at the period when the ethic of individualism was taking hold of society which, as Tawney has analysed in *Religion and the Rise of Capitalism*, was an essential ingredient of that free enterprise capitalism of which the United States is the ultimate expression. Hobbes was describing in theory the very society that Fuller is experiencing.

The setting of Fuller's movies are as bleak as the world of Samuel Beckett – a perfect objective correlative of the Hobbesian state of nature. We first see Zack in *The Steel Helmet* crawling through a field of corpses. He soon joins up with a patrol wandering in a mist-shrouded jungle. They do not know where their lines are nor where the enemy is. They are being shot at by snipers hidden in the trees. In *Fixed Bayonets* the men are holed up in a cave in the midst of a harsh snow-covered wilderness; outside in the snow North Koreans

silently knife you in the back even when you're keeping the keenest watch. In the cave there is a deep hidden drop on one side, stalactites hit you on the head, and one stray bullet can kill anyone inside by its ricochet. *Forty Guns* opens on a bare dusty plain, a heath as blasted as any in *Macbeth* or *Lear*, and the central love scene takes place on this same plain in a lonely ruined shack in the midst of a howling dust-storm. Merrill's marauders fight their way through swamp and jungle behind enemy lines. There may be a machine-gun post round every bend; every man must be in a state of perpetual alert. Half-starved, the men have to leave a parachute drop of food because it will attract the enemy to them. The one man who succumbs to his appetite is killed. They end their odyssey in a stony water-filled shell crater, defending themselves against an enemy who crawls silently and unexpectedly out of the night to slit their throats. In a key moment of action they fight

A bleak world: *Pickup on South Street* (above, left); the field of corpses in *The Steel Helmet*; *Fixed Bayonets*

their way through a tank-trap at Shadzup. This sequence is perhaps the most concentrated expression of the Fuller world. Physically exhausted, the men force their way with sudden bursts of energy, rushing and twisting through a crazy concrete maze. All sense of direction is lost. People are shooting at each other from every angle. Fuller's original conception, which he was not allowed to carry out because it was thought it would be bad for US morale, was even bleaker than the scene we have: he wanted Merrill's men to be killing each other. Only at the end of the action do we crane round and up to see how narrow the maze actually is and how much effort and life has been expended on so little progress.

The tank-trap sequence is the final and complete development of similar sequences, such as the raid on the factory in *House of Bamboo* and the fight among the rocks and caves in *Hell and High Water*. The trek through the jungle had already been sketched out in *China Gate*. It is a world of nightmare in which the mercenaries silently thread their way past sentries and booby-traps, assailed by sudden bursts of vicious machine-gun fire, and where even the innocent eyes of a child are dangerous. Another typical image is the ruined town from which the men set out and to which they return: a town in which the inhabitants starve amid the ruins. We find a similar setting at the beginning of *Verboten*: the hero fights his way through the streets of a ruined town, losing his two companions on the way, himself being wounded but finding love at the end. Outside the specific war setting, Fuller's protagonists also inhabit a bleak world, the dark alleys and back streets of *The Crimson Kimono*, *Pickup on South Street* and *Underworld USA*, or the bleached-out walls and corridors of the mental hospital in *Shock Corridor*.

Fuller himself fought as an infantryman with the Big Red One, First US Infantry Division, from Africa to Czechoslovakia. In terms of his films this was clearly the central experience of his life; he has for a long time wanted to make a movie called *The Big Red One*, his ultimate war movie for

The Big Red One

which all the others are but working sketches. So far he hasn't
managed to set it up. He still uses a Zippo lighter with a big
red one emblazoned on it. But the names of men in his outfit,
such as Lemchek, recur in his films and he gives the line about
fighting from Africa to Czechoslovakia to several of his
characters. Even before his experience of conventional war,
he had known at first hand that other war: crime. During his
most impressionable years he was living in daily contact with
murderers and racketeers. These two experiences colour all
his work.

To measure the desperation of Fuller's films and his view
that film and life are battlefields, we only have to listen to his
views on war. He sees nothing glorious or heroic in it: war is
organized lunacy. As he said in a TV interview with *Cahiers du
Cinéma* in 1967: 'I believe there is nothing more uplifting than
peace, there's nothing uplifting about war. War is tragic. I

don't know anyone who, having fought a war, wants to start again. No one. My films are very anti-war. I don't praise war in my films, I show that it is something barbarous, cannibal, medieval. I don't believe in the so-called rules of war. There is the Geneva Convention, this convention, that convention – it doesn't mean a thing. When two men find themselves face to face and only one will survive, there are no more laws.' It is this basic situation that seems to be at the heart of what Fuller has called his obsession with war. It is in fact a fascination with death. This fascination reveals the inevitably Faustian nature of individualism. For Fuller's heroes, 'the only life-giving answer is to accept the terms of death, to live with death as immediate danger'. As Mailer wrote, in *The Presidential Papers*, of Hemingway's death: 'It may be said he took his life but I wonder if the deed were not more like a reconnaissance from which he did not come back. How likely that he had a death of the most awful proportions within him. He was exactly the one to know that cure for such disease is to risk dying many a time. Somewhere in the deep coma of mortal illness or the transfixed womb of danger, death speaks to us. If we make our way back to life, we are armed with a new secret.' Hence that pull towards suicide in Fuller's movies: Bob Ford in *I Shot Jesse James* willing his own death; Lucky Legs in *China Gate* blowing herself up; Logan in *Forty Guns* hanging himself; Professor Montel in *Hell and High Water* going to an almost certain death; Moe in *Pickup on South Street* forcing the Communist agent to shoot her; the police chief in *Underworld USA* shooting himself; Denno in *Fixed Bayonets* playing a sort of Russian roulette with the minefield. In a way all the men in *Merrill's Marauders* are committing suicide, since their mission is so impossible; certainly Merrill, with his heart condition, is. The threat of suicide hangs like a constant threat over the wards of *Shock Corridor*, where the patients are allowed neither belts nor shoe-laces.

The conflict between a love of and a fear of death is as essential to Fuller's work as the clash between the mercenary and

Suicide: Jeff Chandler as Merrill; Richard Basehart (Denno) carrying Michael O'Shea (Lonergan) through the minefield in *Fixed Bayonets*

the idealist, the rational and the irrational. For survival is at the heart of war, just as it is at the heart of Hobbes's world. Fuller puts it like this: 'We've only one emotion and it's the most important one – death. It's the greatest fear, it's the emotion no one knows anything about, and, regardless of what others assert, it's the only emotion present in every one of us, consciously or unconsciously, twenty-four hours a day. ... Is there a subject greater than death? That's war.' Hobbes expressed it more succinctly: 'Every man shuns death and this he doth by a certain impulsion of nature no less than that whereby a stone moves downwards.' The motive of personal survival is paramount but survival is precarious because, as Hobbes wrote: 'The condition of man ... is a condition of war of everyone against everyone, in which case everyone is governed by his own reason and there is nothing he can make use of that may not be a help unto him, in preserving his life against his enemies; it followeth, that in such a condition every man hath a right to everything; even to one another's body.'

Fuller's movies present this world of constant mutual suspicion. The opening sequence of Fuller's first movie, *I Shot Jesse James*, presents us immediately with one of his most characteristic images: two close-ups of men staring out at us. They look suspiciously at us, at the world, on their guard for the slightest move, but their stares also completely veil their thoughts – we do not know what they are thinking, where they are, who they are. Nor do we know what relationship these two men have to one another. Then, in a medium shot, we see that one is Jesse James, the other a bank cashier whom he is covering with a shotgun. They are two individuals related only by their sense of conflict and their feelings of mutual suspicion. Each knows that the world may blow up in his face at any moment. The cashier's face is a lying mask, completely hiding from Jesse James the fact that his foot is slowly sliding towards an alarm button.

This image of the suspicious and ambiguous look recurs in

64

Fuller's movies. The opening shot of *The Steel Helmet* has the title superimposed over a steel helmet with a bullet hole in it, the conventional image in war movies for death, a symbol of the wastefulness of war. But here, as the titles end the helmet is slowly raised and we see Sergeant Zack's eyes peering out over the top of a bank. All we can see are these suspicious eyes. Our first sight of Zack goes to the heart of his character. Of all Fuller's characters he is the most fully devoted to mere survival; he trusts nothing and no one. *Pickup on South Street* opens with an interplay of conflicting glances that sketches in the main relationships of the film and expresses the lying appearances that are at its centre. Two FBI agents stare at Cuddles. Are they trying to pick her up, or what are they doing? We don't know. Cuddles stares at Skip, who stares back. He is apparently reading a newspaper, but in fact picking her handbag. Skip is being watched but he doesn't know it. Indeed, those watching don't know what is happening until too late. The wounded hero of *Verboten* is saved by a German girl. When he comes to, the first thing we see is a huge close-up of one eye slowly looking around, trying to assess the situation. At the beginning of *Run of the Arrow*, having shot Driscoll, O'Meara looks all round him as he crosses the field towards the body, and as he squats over it, eating, his eyes and head are never at rest. They are like those of an animal over its prey. The first shot of *Underworld USA* is a close-up of Tolly's suspicious eyes, and the first time we see him as an adult his eyes appear over the door of a safe. Tolly's cynical individualism and its basis in his childhood experiences is repeatedly presented in terms of his eyes, the brows quizzically raised, one brow scarred where he was beaten up the night his father died. The Marshal in *Forty Guns* is advised by his friend Griff Bonnell to get out of town because his eyes are failing, and Fuller makes us feel this failure by cutting in subjective out-of-focus shots.

Fuller's characters are right to be watchful, for they wander in a world full of treachery; living, as the existential hero must,

in a perpetual present, they must rely on what is presented to their senses. Their dilemma is that they can rely on nothing but appearances, but appearances lie. And so we find yet another dialectic in Fuller's work, the dialectic expressed in sociological terms by Erving Goffman in *The Presentation of Self in Everyday Life*: 'Underlying all social interaction there seems to be a fundamental dialectic. When one individual enters the presence of others he will want to discover the facts of the situation . . . since the reality that the individual is concerned with is unperceivable at the moment, appearances must be relied upon in its stead. And, paradoxically, the more the individual is concerned with the reality that is not available to perception, the more must he concentrate his attention on appearances.'

There is a scene in *House of Bamboo* which expresses in a concentrated form the dilemma of the Fuller character.

Treachery and the ambiguous look: 'Have you ever seen this man before?' Robert Stack (Spanier) and Shirley Yamaguchi (Mariko) in *House of Bamboo*; and (opposite) Jean Peters in the opening subway sequence in *Pickup on South Street*

Mariko and her uncle kneel quietly on the floor of their house in private conversation; suddenly strange men burst into the room, knock down the uncle and ask Mariko, 'Have you ever seen this man before?' She stares at a man who she thinks is Eddie Spanier, a friend of her late husband. Eddie is trying to track down his killer and revenge him. She had been asked by her husband to keep their marriage a secret and Eddie had told her not to tell anyone she had seen him. Perhaps these men are her husband's killers – she must be careful, she must protect Eddie. So she denies having seen him. But Eddie has told the gang he spent the afternoon with Mariko, when he was in fact seeing colleagues in the police, because he is not really Eddie Spanier but a double agent. So Eddie goes up to Mariko, slaps her hard, accuses her of lying and makes her confess that he was with her that afternoon. So she was right not to tell the truth, but how could she tell which was the correct lie to choose?

In Fuller's movies the shifting layers of treachery are so complex that his characters are almost permanently in such situations. This is I think a particularly American dilemma; in a static conservative society the social roles that people enact do not change much and can easily be checked. In *The Presentation of Self in Everyday Life*, Goffman says: 'Society is organized on the principle that any individual who possesses certain social characteristics has a moral right to expect that others will value and treat him in an appropriate way. Connected with this principle is a second, namely that an individual who implicitly or explicitly signifies that he has certain social characteristics ought in fact to be what he claims he is.' In America in particular, and in modern society in general, such moral certainties have broken down. We are faced with a fluid view of character within a fluid society; the existential hero doesn't after all even know who he is claiming to be.

This confusion of appearance and reality is embedded throughout Fuller's movies. The peasants at a wayside shrine start shooting at Zack and Short Round and turn out to be

The double agent: Robert Stack (Spanier/Kenner) and Robert Ryan (Sandy) in *House of Bamboo*

Shifting loyalties: Sandy interviews Mariko

North Korean soldiers. The body of a dead American soldier
is booby-trapped. Zack insists that they thoroughly search a
column of refugees for arms, for as he says, 'How can you tell
a North Korean from a South Korean? One is running with
you, the other's running after you.' In *Fixed Bayonets* Rock
even mistakes his own bare foot for someone else's. Fuller's
most extended presentation of the appearance/reality confusion is in *House of Bamboo*. When Eddie Spanier first
arrives in Japan he is presented to the audience, as he is to the
gang he has come to infiltrate, as a petty hoodlum. We see the
photograph he shows to Mariko and we take it as genuine. We
see him roughing up *pachinko* parlour operators, we see him
arrested on a phoney charge, and we hear the police department reading out his criminal record. We are presented with
the same information as Sandy, and it is only after Sandy has
been deceived and Eddie is in his gang that we, the audience,

learn that in fact Eddie is an undercover agent. So we are directly involved in the shifting loyalties of the film. The whole movie is based upon such a structure of mutually concealed realities, indeed of shifting levels of reality, so that what was false becomes real. Mariko becomes Eddie's girl friend in order to help him revenge her husband's death, and then by enacting the role actually falls in love with him. Eddie is punched in the *pachinko* parlour and crashes through a thin paper wall to the world of Sandy's gang, for which the parlour is a front. Realities become confused. Eddie, although an Army policeman, acts like a gangster. The gangsters, on the other hand, behave like the Army. Indeed, most of the gang are ex-Army; they use Army weapons, Army strategy and Army language. After Mariko has been out to deliver a message for Eddie to the Army, Sandy interviews her. She has been seen by another member of the gang coming out of a room at the Imperial Hotel, followed shortly afterwards by an American. Significantly this scene is played in a mirror. We assume, as does Mariko, that Sandy is questioning her because he suspects treachery, but he in fact accuses her of disturbing Eddie's peace of mind by cheating on him with other men. Sandy believes her lies and denies her truths. In the same way he saves Eddie, who is betraying him, and he kills Griff, his closest friend, because he wrongly suspects him of treachery.

Such a dialectic of loyalty and treachery recurs in many Fuller movies. In *Verboten* the civilian helpers of the American military government in Germany are really leaders of the neo-Nazi Werewolf organization; the loving fiancée is really marrying the American as a meal ticket, but, to add a further layer of confusion, by the time the American finds this out it is no longer true, as she really loves him. In *Shock Corridor* a journalist pretends to be a madman but, as the movie progresses, we discover that perhaps he is a madman masquerading as a journalist, just as his fellow inmates pretend they are Confederate generals, members of the Ku Klux Klan or five-year-old children. In *The Naked Kiss* a prostitute takes on the

Confusion of identity: Negro Klansman in *Shock Corridor*

role of a nurse while a nurse tries to become a prostitute, and the town's benefactor and war hero is really a child-molester.

But as always in Fuller's world the problem returns to the individual. In *The Crimson Kimono* Joe and Charlie are both in love with the same girl. It is significant that Joe's true feelings of antagonism to Charlie are expressed during a *kendo* bout when both are wearing masks. *Kendo* represents a ritualized form of self-control. It is here used to embody society and social pressure. It has obvious similarities to the rules of war that Fuller so much dislikes. The strength of Joe's feelings breaks out from behind the mask, he becomes really violent and actually hurts Charlie. In this scene Fuller expresses the same conflict between the individual and society that Goffman defines: 'The expressive coherence that is required in performances points out a crucial discrepancy between our all-too-human selves and our socialized selves.

As human beings we are presumably creatures of variable impulse with moods and energies that change from one moment to the next. As characters put on for an audience, however, we must not be subject to ups and downs. As Durkheim suggested, we do not allow our higher social activity "to follow in the trail of our bodily states as our sensations and our general bodily consciousness do".' (*The Presentation of Self in Everyday Life.*)

For Fuller a meaningful society can only arise out of the fullest expression of self. 'Without liberty life wouldn't be worth living.' One of the deep ironies of his movies is that the will to survive can so easily become a denial of self. In the character of Zack Fuller examines the limitations of a mere desire to survive. Zack, faced by the complexities which, as we have seen, the visible world presents, retreats behind a cynicism as restrictive as any social pressures. Zack is pure survival, basic individualism. In the second shot of *The Steel Helmet*, wounded in one leg, his arms tied behind his back, he crawls through a field of corpses. The camera pulls back in front and slightly above him, and we are immediately involved in the sheer physical effort of survival. When he is cut free by Short Round, the South Korean orphan, he immediately starts tending his wounds without a word. Not until he has dealt with the priorities of physical survival has he any time for human relationships; even then he immediately wants to disengage. He wants to cancel his debt to Short Round by giving him chocolate to keep the relationship on a strictly mercenary level, where no loyalties are involved. But he hasn't any chocolate to give. When Short Round starts to follow him, Zack tells him to go away. Then Short Round says to him, 'When you save someone's life his heart is in your hands.' With this phrase we are straight into one of Fuller's central paradoxes: the prime responsibility is to oneself, and yet no man is an island. We need other people. Whether Zack likes it or not, Short Round has probably saved his life. So Zack tells him grudgingly, 'You can come along but you're on your own', a phrase that could serve as a motto for all Fuller's movies.

Zack's individualism is expressed in directly physical terms. On meeting the medic he immediately asks for a bar of chocolate to liquidate his debt to Short Round: he agrees to lead the patrol to the temple for a box of stogies. The connection between his physical appetite and his cynicism is conveyed in the scene with the booby-trapped corpse. Zack is sitting with the patrol guzzling water-melons, the close-up high angle in which he is seen accentuating the animality of his eating. We are reminded that Fuller condemns war for turning men into animals. One of the GIs reports that he has found a dead American: the Lieutenant tells him to get his dog-tag. Zack says: 'Leave him, a dead man is a dead man, nobody cares.' He is totally unsentimental and appears to us as brutally callous, but when the GI goes to fetch the dog-tag he is blown up by the booby-trapped body. Zack, his mouth full of melon, sneeringly remarks, 'Get his dog-tag, big deal.' We see that his cynicism is completely realistic in this context, essential to his survival. But this is seen as a condemnation of the context, for we see also that only by denying his feelings, by making himself a less complete individual, can he survive. The process of breaking down his narrow individualism begins when he looks with bemused fascination at the prayer-drums that Short Round has been turning. Earlier he had derisively dismissed the prayer that Short Round had pinned to his back, ripping it off as though it were some foul disease. Zack finally admits an emotional attachment to Short Round by making out a dog-tag for him on the same table and with the same pen that Short Round has just used to write a prayer. The two actions are directly equated visually. But as so often in Fuller's movies such a moment of tenderness and relaxation is followed immediately by an attack. Once a chink shows in the armour of self, life instantly exploits it. So at the moment Zack admits love to himself, Short Round is shot. His reaction, the shooting of the North Korean Major, is the start

The Steel Helmet: Zack meets the medic

of his madness. He accepts values outside his immediate needs, becomes less ruthless, less cynical, less limited, but in so doing becomes vulnerable to the pressures of war and is destroyed.

Time and again on the battleground of his movies Fuller relentlessly forces the audience to face the centrally tragic absurdity of individualism. We are never allowed to forget 'the absolutely devaluing limit of death'. The power and desperation of these movies comes out of the conflict between the individual and his environment. It is a tragic conflict because the individual creates the very environment that destroys him. A religion of individualism inevitably creates a state of war in which the individual is perpetually threatened. And so the liberty of the Fuller protagonist is 'sheer will, sheer tension'. Under the ever-present shadow of death he is

75

heir to that tradition of Faustian defiance which, as Fiedler has shown, is central to classic American literature from Hawthorne to Faulkner.

3: Fuller and Love

Fuller uses the central relationship of our civilization, the one between a man and a woman, to personalize and internalize all the conflicts and tensions, all the incompatible drives and paradoxes of modern society. He specifically links the love theme in his movies to his view of the world as a battlefield. Jessica Drummond says to Griff Bonnell in *Forty Guns* that love 'is like war, easy to start and hard to stop.' Joe says to Chris in *The Crimson Kimono*, 'Let's not set off a bomb.' Fuller is able to examine all the themes in his work in terms of love, because love is the extreme expression of the basic polarity underlying all his movies; irrational personal desire and obsession with self, and at the same time denial of self in an involvement with and allegiance to another.

The friendship between Joe and Charlie in *The Crimson Kimono* blossoms in a foxhole, and we have a feeling with all Fuller's love-affairs that they are taking place under fire. Sometimes this is true in the most literal sense: Brock and Lucky Legs in *China Gate* work out the conflicts in their marriage while on a mission behind enemy lines – it begins with a slap and ends with a huge explosion. The hero of *Verboten* meets his wife while fighting his way through the streets of a German town; Adam Jones in *Hell and High Water* falls in love with Professor Montel's daughter in a submarine on a secret mission in Arctic waters. And their first kiss takes place

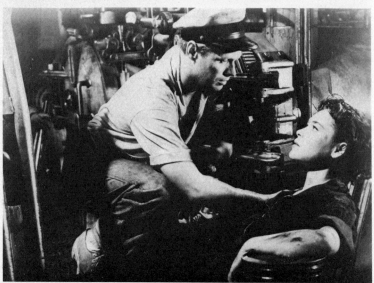

Lovers under fire: Angie Dickinson (Lucky Legs) and Brock (Gene Barry) in *China Gate*; Richard Widmark (Adam Jones) and Bella Darvi (Denise Gerard) in *Hell and High Water*

as the submarine lies on the bottom, leaking and short of air, trying to escape a tracking enemy submarine. Their relationship develops in a fight among the caves and rocks of a bleak enemy-occupied island. When O'Meara meets Yellow Moccasin he is being pursued on the Run and having arrows fired at him. When actual war conditions are absent the relationships still take place in the midst of conflicts. Candy and Skip are caught in the middle of a fight between Communist agents and the FBI; they are liable to be arrested, beaten up or shot at at any moment. Tolly meets Cuddles as she is being beaten up by a hoodlum in the back room of a coffee-bar off a dark alley. Their love, like Skip and Candy's, is caught in the cross-fire of the FBI and the Syndicate. In *The Crimson Kimono* Chris, Joe and Charlie work out the cross-currents of their triangular relationship in the midst of a murder investigation, during which Chris is shot at by the murderess and both Joe and Charlie are under constant threat of physical violence at the hands of petty criminals. Eddie Spanier/Sergeant Kenner and Mariko in *House of Bamboo* develop their affair in the house of the man they are betraying, under constant threat of discovery and death.

There is a notable absence of soft lights and sweet music in Fuller romances. They are conducted against the harshest of backgrounds: subway trains, the damp hard wooden slats of a waterfront pier, and a hospital bed are the setting for Skip and Candy's romance. Tolly and Cuddles meet in deserted garbage-filled alleys, on park benches and in anonymous claustrophobic flats; Barrett and Cathy see their love destroyed in strip clubs and the harsh, glaring, featureless wards of a mental hospital; the hero of *Verboten* and his wife live in a wrecked house in a bombed, starving town. These affairs, when they are working – and that isn't often, for conflict is seen as the basis of love, as of all other relationships – are fragile, threatened oases in the midst of a harsh chaos. They are like the scene in the native village in *Merrill's Marauders*, a time for the mutual binding of wounds. It is not only the

Hell and High Water

wounds of the soldiers that are tended, but also those of the native girl. Against a background of a general state of war the smallest gesture of solidarity and comfort becomes unbearably beautiful. When the old lady feeds the tough, grizzled sergeant with a small bowl of rice he bursts into tears.

The motif of tending wounds recurs in the presentation of many Fuller love-affairs. In *Hell and High Water* Adam Jones tenderly bathes the bruises on the face of Miss Montel; in *House of Bamboo* Mariko massages Sergeant Kenner's neck after he has been shot; in *Run of the Arrow* Yellow Moccasin binds O'Meara's feet and sweats out his fever; in *Verboten* the whole relationship starts with Helga putting the unconscious American soldier to bed and dressing his wounds. In *Underworld USA*, similarly, Tolly saves Cuddles from a beating-up, and in their first scenes together we see Tolly bathing her cut cheek. Even where there is not a direct tending of wounds the images of wounds are associated with love. Skip realizes his love for Candy when he sees her bruised and beaten face looking up at him from a hospital bed. In *Shock Corridor* Cathy fondles Johnny's bandaged head when she visits him in the mental hospital. In Fuller's concept of love there is something of the Nietzschean relaxation of the warrior. But the Fuller warrior must never relax. Love is seen as a fatal trap, into which men and women are drawn by irresistible and irrational forces. So Fuller's protagonists – men and women alike – are always suspicious of love.

When I say that the Fuller concept of love is the relaxation of the warrior, I do not imply, as the Nietzschean view does, any idea of male superiority. In Fuller movies the men and women are all warriors; in this respect Fuller is more mature than Hawks. The Fuller hero and the Hawks hero share the same suspicion of involvement, the same desire to keep their guard up. But the Hawks woman, unlike the Fuller woman, does not share that suspicion: the Hawks woman is independent and proud of it, sure, but she is always seen as an outsider in an essentially male environment. The woman, in *Only Angels Have Wings*, *Rio Bravo* or *Hatari*, is put through tests to see if she is acceptable in male terms. Although it is true, especially at the end of *Rio Bravo*, that women do represent for Hawks a balance and complexity lacking in the purely male world of his heroes, he never faces the implications of that balance and complexity. In Fuller they are faced head on: Fuller characters are driven by such powerful desires that they rush to the very heart of these complexities. The Hawks hero has a strong homosexual streak and feels that he could very well do without women altogether. Neither the Fuller hero nor the Fuller heroine can do without each other. That's the basis for their mutual drama. Hawks is examining a traditional world in which women are half emancipated: whatever her apparent independence, we feel that Feathers in *Rio Bravo* will wait around for Chance. Fuller heroines could not wait around for Fuller heroes even if they wanted to – their drives

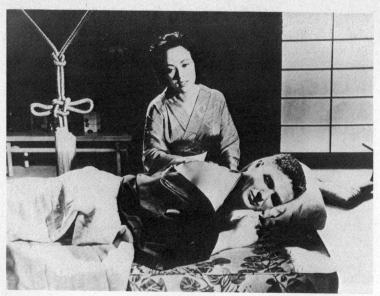

Tending wounds: *House of Bamboo*; and *Pickup on South Street*

Shock Corridor (Constance Towers as Cathy, with Barrett); and *Underworld USA* (Cliff Robertson as Tolly with Dolores Dean as Cuddles)

are as powerful and conflicting as those of the male.

Increasingly, as Fuller's work develops, the women are seen to be the stronger characters. Lucky Legs fights to support the son Brock has deserted, leads the expedition to its objective, and finally accomplishes its task. Candy in *Pickup on South Street* knocks Skip out so that she rather than he can run the risk of confronting the Communist agent; Montel's daughter in *Hell and High Water* is completely equipped as linguist and scientist to take over her father's role. Charity Hackett runs the biggest newspaper on Park Row; Jessica Drummond in *Forty Guns* has built up a huge spread and completely dominates Cochise County financially, politically and sexually, the forty gunmen doing her bidding; Helga in *Verboten* is the sole supporter of her invalid mother and her brother and can still find the time and energy to dress the hero's wounds and hide him from the SS. Chris in *The Crimson Kimono* quite willingly takes on the risks of helping to identify the murder suspect, and is much tougher and more clear-headed about her difficult relationship with Charlie and Joe than either of the two men. In *Shock Corridor* Cathy works as a singer in a striptease club to support Johnny, and she is the only one who appears concerned about the pervasive madness and corruption in the film. *The Naked Kiss* opens with Kelly knocking out and robbing a man; she works the small towns as a prostitute to be free of any pimp. Having decided for personal reasons to give up prostitution she becomes a successful and hard-working nurse. She is the person people turn to for help; she stops one nurse from becoming a prostitute, and gives another money to have her baby. When she discovers her fiancé molesting a child she kills him. Cleared of the murder she eventually leaves town, disgusted, to go back to prostitution. The only men in the film are weak, corrupt and hypocritical: a pimp, a war hero who is really a sexual pervert, and a police chief who enjoys the prostitute's favours but who will only let her work across the river outside his town.

Shock Corridor: Cathy at the striptease club

Women represent not just a haven but sanity. Cynthy in
I Shot Jesse James bitterly criticizes Jesse for what a life of
crime is doing to his wife; and to Bob Ford she represents a
quiet domestic life as a farmer. The tragedy is that Bob can
only attain this ideal by murdering Jesse, and the murder
disgusts Cynthy. It is Reavis's young child-bride who persuades him to give up his mad dream to become baron of
Arizona; at the end she meets him as he comes out of prison
and, looking down from the carriage, simply says: 'Get in.'
Cuddles in *Underworld USA* is prepared, at great danger to
herself, to help society by testifying against the Syndicate,
which makes Tolly regard her as a sucker. Her remark to him,
'We've got a right to climb out of the sewer and live like other
people', is echoed by Cathy, in *Shock Corridor*, who tells
Johnny, in an effort to dissuade him from his mad scheme,

Orphans: Ty Hardin (*Merrill's Marauders*); Warren Hsieh (*China Gate*)

'I'm saving so that we can have a normal life.' O'Meara's mother tells him that he is sick; Moe tells Skip to 'stop using your hands and start using your head'; Sandy tells Tolly that he is a midget. The pessimism of Fuller's films lies in their demonstration of the fact that the normal sane life dreamed of by women is impossible.

Because of this failure, family life, which is seen as centred on the figure of the woman as mother, is impossible. Without families children become delinquents; a vicious circle of endless corruption begins. In the work of Kazan and Nicholas Ray, the directors whose movies are closest to Fuller's in their analysis of contemporary American life, we see the family as it breaks up. In *Rebel Without a Cause* and *East of Eden*, *The Lusty Men* and *Splendour in the Grass*, the fabric of families and marriages is in the process of being torn apart by the pressures of modern society, its restless mobility, its quests for money or success or sexual satisfaction, its inherent selfishness. In Fuller's movies we see the aftermath of this process of disillusion, just as so often we see the aftermath of war. Hence the prevalence of orphans: the girl in *The Baron of Arizona* is thought to be an orphan, Short Round in *The Steel Helmet* is one; so, too, are Jessica Drummond in *Forty Guns*, Silent Tongue in *Run of the Arrow*, Tolly in *Underworld USA*, Stock in *Merrill's Marauders*. In *The Naked Kiss* Kelly works in an orphanage. Even when they are not orphans they are actually or potentially fatherless, like Lucky Legs's son in *China Gate*, Helga and her brother in *Verboten*. In *Forty Guns* and *Underworld USA* the loss of the father is violent – Jessica recounts how her father was killed trying to defend her from a drunken cowhand; Tolly witnesses the murder of his own father. This absence of fathers is associated with the frustration of the natural desire to have and bring up children; Sandy in *Underworld USA* is surrounded by photographs of children and huge clockwork dolls, symbols of the children she could never have. In *The Naked Kiss* Kelly is infertile. Goldie's wife in *China Gate* couldn't have children: 'I've always wanted a child, Brock, especially a five-year-old one.' The destruction of normal family life is felt as one of the many frustrations in Fuller's world. The extreme case of this frustration is Brock, who rejects his own child.

The fatherless or parentless children are driven by their environment into delinquency. It is the only way they can survive the pressures of war. So Short Round is already at home with the names of US Army weapons. He is dressed in ill-fitting US Army uniform. Tolly becomes a revenge-maddened hoodlum; Skip and Candy in *Pickup on South Street* we feel to be orphans in their prime, baring their fangs at the world to hide their wounds. Helga's brother joins the Werewolf; the orphans in *The Naked Kiss* are actually crippled and can act as pirates only in fantasy games. Children, whether orphans or not, are under continual threat: the final shoot-out in *House of Bamboo* takes place in a children's playground, and the most horrifying moment in *Underworld USA*, a movie packed with violence, is the killing of a child by the Syndicate torpedo, Gus. The children in *The Naked Kiss* are sexually assaulted by the most respectable man in town; Stuart in *Shock Corridor* becomes a renegade GI in Korea because his pappy gave him 'no knowledge of my country, just a hymn of hate'.

The lapsed responsibilities of parenthood are often taken on by other people; indeed, the ability to do this is seen as a sign of maturity and health. Appropriately, in an existential world not even parenthood is forced upon people – it must be consciously assumed. Reavis adopts the young orphan girl, Zack looks after Short Round, Brock takes on responsibility for his rejected son, the responsibility Goldie had said he would take on. 'Your son will go to America if I have to crawl all the way there with him on my back.' Silent Tongue is saved from the quicksand by a US cavalry trooper at the cost of his life and is adopted by Yellow Moccasin and O'Meara. Merrill adopts Stock by letting him write letters to his family because he hasn't one of his own; Sandy acts as a mother to

Tolly and Cuddles, just as Moe acts as a mother to Skip, a fact he recognizes when he gives her a decent burial. Kelly becomes mother to a whole crowd of crippled orphans.

In *China Gate* and *Verboten* this concept of taking a voluntary responsibility for people is transferred to the United States. In *Verboten* the hero is responsible, as an employee of the US military government, for feeding the Germans – in a world of scarcity this is the primary act of protection. Images of scarcity abound in Fuller's movies: the first thing Zack wants to give Short Round is chocolate; *China Gate* opens with Lucky Legs's son scavenging for food for his puppy and being pursued by a man with a knife who wants to eat the dog. This is immediately followed by a US food-drop. *Run of the Arrow* opens with O'Meara gnawing at food taken from the pockets of a soldier he has just shot. Merrill's marauders slowly starve as they trek through the jungle, lack of food sending one man mad. In *Verboten* civilians scrabble for a few spilt potatoes, and Helga tells her German boy friend that she regards her American husband as a meal ticket.

So the orphan motif and the theme of substitute parenthood merge with the theme of national identity. In a sense all Americans are orphans because they have rejected the culture and society from which they came; fleeing from Europe or Asia, they have destroyed their own fathers in order to become 'new men, masterless men'. The trauma of this immigrant adaptation to American society is recorded in the Jewish novel, with its recurrent theme of escape from dominant parents. This experience is also shared by the blacks. They live in a matriarchal society, their fathers castrated by prejudice and oppression, and can only regain pride in themselves by rejecting the culture imposed on them by their white masters. Malcolm X, for instance, was not literally an orphan. But, in his autobiography, there is the feeling of a man willing himself to become one. Fuller sees the solution to this problem in the very fact that America is so formless, so rootless culturally that it can be the prototype for a world society into which all races could be absorbed. The message of his movies is that America can become the father and mother of us all, not by pretending to unity but by accepting its own heterogeneous nature, all its conflicts and confusions. That would seem to be the only dream of America worth pursuing.

Fuller's men and women meet each other as they meet the world, full of suspicion. They face up to each other like two wary boxers, often literally beginning their relationship with a physical fight, so that their relationship becomes a microcosm for war and of life. The first time Spanier/Kenner meets Mariko he pursues her through the streets and wrestles her to the floor of her room. The second time he slaps her hard across the face. The first time Skip meets Candy he steals her wallet. The next time he starts by knocking her down and picking her purse again, and ends the meeting by knocking her about, throwing her out of his shack and tossing her handbag after her. *The Naked Kiss* opens with a violent fight between a man and a woman. The reason for these fights lies in the individual's basic responsibility to self in a world of whose motives he or she is intensely suspicious. The most concrete expression of this clash between the primacy of self and any relationship are the screens in *House of Bamboo*: here the props of the Japanese setting are beautifully used to express the essential aloneness of Fuller's characters. Sometimes dialogue scenes are played through the slit bamboo screens that separate their sleeping pallets; sometimes a scene ends with Mariko lowering the screen between them. The relationship of those screens, physical or metaphorical, to vulnerability is shown in the scene where Spanier/Kenner takes a bath; it was he who suggested that Mariko should move in with him as his *kimono* to help fool the gang, but in the bath scene he is suddenly made aware of the implications of his act. His embarrassment covers an awareness of the physical and emotional complications of this relationship and of any relationship. The screens he puts round himself, the

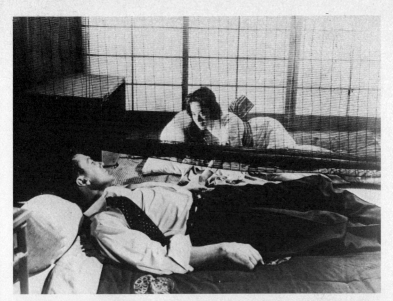

House of Bamboo: screens; and the shooting of Griff (Cameron Mitchell)

fact that the water is too hot, the difficulty of eating poached eggs with chopsticks, are all used to underline the uncomfortable nature of his relationship to Mariko, based as it is from the outset on treachery, on appearances rather than reality.

Fuller uses baths as recurring vulnerability images: later in *House of Bamboo* Griff is killed by Sandy as he sits in a bath. The scene is played in one shot; we see the bullets ripping holes in the bath and we feel physically what they are doing to Griff's naked body. Then as the scene progresses, the water running out of the holes emphasizes not only the ebbing of Griff's life but also the fluidity of life, its lack of moral certainty. We know that Griff has not betrayed Sandy and yet Sandy's incantations, as he holds Griff's head – 'I'm right, I always am' – merge with the sound of running water into a powerfully ironic image of the fragility of human relationships; relationships destroyed not wilfully but by the conditions of life itself. This bath image is also used in *Forty Guns* for much the same purpose.

In *House of Bamboo* the screens are actually there in a physical sense, but screens of emotion are always there in Fuller movies. They may be racial as well, as in *China Gate*, *The Crimson Kimono* and *House of Bamboo*; Fuller uses his emotional relationships to examine the colour problem, but he also uses racial and cultural differences to examine the moral problems of any relationship by stressing the otherness of people. So it is not really the fact that she is Japanese that keeps Mariko apart from Kenner, but rather the fact that she is an individual with different experiences and needs. In that sense each one of us is a member of a different race; so in *The Crimson Kimono* it is a shared experience of art that brings Chris and Joe together, it is Joe's shared experience of war with Charlie that constitutes the barrier between Chris and Joe. Race is only a pretext, as the movie makes clear.

But before experiences can be shared a thicket of mutual suspicion must be cleared. In the love-affairs Fuller concen-

'Not everybody wears their lives on their faces': the French colonel and Lucky Legs in *China Gate*

trates all the tensions inherent in the confusion of appearance and reality that pervades his world; men and women meet as total strangers; thrown temporarily together, they know nothing about each other, they must learn from what they see and hear. And this is always hugely difficult, for, as Lucky Legs says, 'not everybody wears their lives on their faces'. Indeed, because of that general structure of treachery in which they are involved, Fuller's characters are struggling not to wear their lives on their faces. To show your real self can make you vulnerable. The ironies of this dialectic between a real and assumed self are seen in *The Naked Kiss*. Miss Josephine the seamstress says to Kelly, 'Your reference is that face, Miss Kelly', implying that her face expresses goodness. We know that she was a prostitute – in the opening scene of the film she turned towards the camera as if it were a mirror and carefully made up the face we see, constructing it like an actor

'Your reference is that face, Miss Kelly' – Constance Towers (Kelly) and Anthony Eisley (Griff) in *The Naked Kiss*

building up his make-up before a performance, its artificiality stressed by the fact that we have seen her bald and the hair is a wig. But the irony is not simple – Fuller's world has more complexity than that. For we also know that Kelly is in fact good, that her physical presence as a prostitute masks an essential inner moral worth. The final irony is that her mask of respectability enables her to find her dream man, the local hero and philanthropist. She decides to trust him and tells him about her past – she rips off the mask and apparently that act of honesty pays. She was right to trust him, he wants to marry her in spite of everything. They have found, we think, a relationship based on profound personal honesty; but no – for the man wears a mask as well – beneath the cultured philanthropist and war hero lurks a sexual pervert. It is just because she was a prostitute that he wants to marry her. The depths of treachery possible in human relationships are summed up as he goes down on his knees to Kelly and says: 'Our life will be a paradise because we are both abnormal.'

This pattern of treachery is common to many of Fuller's

love relationships. Fuller films love scenes like a patrol in a booby-trapped, sniper-filled no man's land. Candy and Skip kiss and cuddle on the New York waterfront. The setting may be sordid but the expressions of mutual affection, or at any rate desire, look genuine enough. In fact, Candy is trying to get some microfilm off Skip for her ex-boy friend, and Skip is intent on using her as a go-between to obtain the best price he can for his film. Tolly rescues Cuddles; then, in a particularly brutal pseudo-love scene, tends her wounds, not out of affection but in order to prise Gus's telephone number out of her. The number will help him get his revenge. As Victor Perkins has pointed out, he repeats it to himself 'as eagerly as if the numbers were cherished words of love'. Cuddles's attempts at affection or suggestions of marriage are repulsed with violent ridicule: 'Marry? Marry you?'

There is one sequence in *Verboten* which, by containing two opposing emotional truths, brilliantly expresses the treachery feared by the Fuller hero. Brent tells Helga that the US Army has released him. Now he can marry her. They kiss, and he goes off. As they kiss we see a German soldier staggering slowly towards them down a street in the background; when Brent has gone he greets Helga and she helps him into the house. In the next shot inside the house Helga tells the German soldier, Bruno, a rabid Nazi, that Brent is just a meal ticket. But once again the situation is not as simple as it seems: simple treachery is no more possible than simple loyalty. The moral complexity of Fuller's movies is part of their modernity. We are far here from the calm moral assurance of Hawks or Ford. When Brent loses his job and so will no longer be able to provide for Helga, Bruno tells him, pretending to be friendly, that of course Helga will now leave him because she only married him as a meal ticket. He storms home and tells Helga it is finished, he won't be taken for a sucker any more. But in Fuller's world everything is in constant motion. His characters must live in the present. They may be making as big a mistake about treachery as about loyalty: Helga points out that yes, of course she married him as a meal ticket, what else could she do? She didn't know him as anything else. But after living with him she genuinely loves him. But Brent will not listen: 'I couldn't believe you no matter what you tell me and you know why? Because I'm up to my neck in double-crosses in this damn country.'

In such a world of double-crosses it is action that must be relied upon. Loyalty or affection cannot be talked about, it can only be demonstrated. When at the beginning of *Verboten* Brent asks Helga: 'Why are you sticking your neck out for me?', she replies, 'I will show you there is a difference between a Nazi and a German.' Helga demonstrates this and reunites herself with Brent by taking her brother to see the War Crimes Tribunal at Nuremberg. Candy demonstrates her love for Skip by risking death at the hands of the Communist agent rather than give him Skip's address. Skip demonstrates his love for Candy by pursuing and beating up the Communist agent. Cuddles shows her love for Tolly by sticking her neck out and agreeing to testify against the Syndicate. Tolly shows his love for Cuddles by killing Gus and Connors.

The atmosphere of suspicion is so all-pervading that a character has to be forced into such an act of commitment. The existential hero discovers the meaning of his life in a process of enactment; love is seen as so irrational, so impossible, that one can only be trapped into it by circumstances. Mariko and Spanier/Kenner begin by acting out a love-affair; by so doing they come to love one another. Candy and Skip do the same – it is when people's individual paths happen to run parallel that some sort of love is possible. But individualism must come first. So Lucky Legs and Brock are involved in an expedition to blow up a Communist ammunition-dump. They have different reasons for going on the expedition, but it brings them together. The same is true of the murder investigation in *The Crimson Kimono*. Tolly and Cuddles happen to need each other at different times and for different reasons. So do Brent and Helga, in *Verboten*.

Run of the Arrow: Sarita Montiel (Yellow Moccasin) and Rod Steiger (O'Meara)

Life can conspire either for or against the relationship, but even when it is conspiring for it the acts of commitment to which such relationships lead are seen as inherently dangerous, even fatal. Love and death are closely linked in Fuller's films, as they have been in romantic literature, as they are deeply in America's myths. Love means the death of individuality, love is both the highest expression of individualism and also its violation. The concept of romantic love is based upon frustration, upon the idea that the structure of society makes such a love impossible and that if the love is fulfilled the lovers will be punished as transgressors. America is a society based more and more on self, on individualism, and in this sense America is the most romantic of societies, purely a product of the Romantic era. In such a society love comes to be seen as a transgression of the self. So love is a trap, a relaxation of the tensions which keep the self together and protect it from the

97

destructive pressures surrounding it. This idea is most vividly expressed in *Verboten*: Brent fights his way through the streets with two fellow GIs; the sequence illustrates a basic drive forward, and the rapid tracking shots with Beethoven's music embody restless pulsating energy. But it is not a smooth, flowing, relaxed energy – the movements of the men and cameras are jagged, they stop and start, zig-zagging to avoid bullets. Brent loses his companions one after the other as he dodges his way deeper into the town. He cannot relax his vigilance for an instant or he too will be shot. He is in fact wounded but goes on to outwit a German sniper – he doesn't just shoot him. Even when trapped in a railway wagon, the German might have tricked his way out against someone less alert than Brent. Finally, Brent bursts into a house and sees Helga standing in front of him – he immediately falls to the floor unconscious. The sight of a woman is linked to the idea of safety, and his drive to keep going evaporates. A similar reaction can be seen in *Shock Corridor*, where achievement of his goal leads to Johnny Barrett's mental breakdown. Woman, the satisfaction of basic male drives, the orgasm, are linked with madness, with the final destruction of all social constraints, the dissolution of self.

Marriage is directly linked with death. In *Forty Guns* as Wes falls to the ground shot, his bride's wedding-dress and veil cover the body. This image is repeated in *The Naked Kiss*. When Kelly discovers Grant with the little girl, she is carrying her wedding-dress in a carton. As she kills him she drops the box and the wedding-veil falls over his dead upturned face. In the previous sequence at Miss Josephine's house we have seen the wedding-dress on the dressmaker's dummy, an effigy of Miss Josephine's dead fiancé. There is a further use of the image of a white veil falling over a dead body. When Chowhound in *Merrill's Marauders* is machine-gunned as he goes for food dropped by air, a flapping white parachute falls over his body, and the sequence ends. Thus the marriage-as-death imagery is linked to the fact of Chowhound succumbing

Sex, madness and destruction: Barrett and nymphomaniacs in *Shock Corridor*; the opening of *Forty Guns*

to his physical appetite. It is the awareness of the power of desire and passion that makes marriage so dangerous. In *House of Bamboo* Weber's marriage to Mariko is revealed to us as he dies on an operating-table – Weber has told Mariko to keep their marriage a secret and Eddie Spanier advises her to do the same. To admit that you are married is to admit a loyalty to another person and so a vulnerability that can be exploited. The fact that marriage is a doomed attempt to deny the self is stressed in *Run of the Arrow*: here the marriage ceremony is presented as the high point of O'Meara's absorption into the Sioux nation, the moment when he agrees to kill Americans if they are enemies of the Sioux. Though Yellow Moccasin stays with O'Meara, we must doubt the stability of this union, for the end of the film is an affirmation of just those deeper loyalties which O'Meara's marriage has attempted to deny; and the scene in which Yellow Moccasin points out to O'Meara that his killing of Driscoll shows he can never be a Sioux is written and played as a key moment in the break-up of a marriage.

The themes of love and death, marriage and death, sex and violence, are given their most original and powerful treatment in *Forty Guns*. This is the Fuller movie about which it is hardest to write because more than any other it is pure experience, pure movie. From the opening sequence we are plunged into a world presented in terms of interacting images of animal energy and violation; the visual and aural rhythms of the opening sequence present the clash of two sexual drives, a mutual rape. As Jessica Drummond and her forty horsemen sweep past the Bonnell brothers in their wagon, hooves pound, dust swirls, horses rear and whinny, and the whole is tied together by a crucial phallic crane shot as the wagon appears to plunge up between the two lines of horses. Then the camera sinks until it is we, the audience, who are tearing straight into the turmoil. Out of this violent clash comes the intimate connection in Fuller's work, as in American society, between sex and violence, and in particular between sex and guns, the ultimate expression of frontier virility. This connection was examined in a more contemporary setting in Penn's *The Chase*, particularly in the drunken party sequence; it is also the central theme of Mailer's *Why Are We In Vietnam*? The obsessive cataloguing of guns in that book is close in intention and tone to Fuller's use of guns in *Forty Guns*: the pistol and the rifle are recurring phallic symbols in both dialogue and image. Brock's wilful and pointless shooting of the Marshal and then his shooting-up of the town are linked to his sexual irresponsibility, which is itself seen as an example of untamed natural forces. After the shoot-up in the town Jessica takes away Brock's guns, and then in the same dialogue sequence upbraids him for spawning bastards with every girl in the neighbourhood, 'leaving a calf in every corral'. She leaves him with the words: 'If you can't handle a horse without spurs you have no business riding.'

When Griff confronts Brock in the street it is seen as a straight clash between two virilities, ending with a track-in to Brock's unraised gun. We realize later that Griff represents the father Brock has never had; the whole action of the film from that moment can be seen as the working out of a classic Oedipus complex.

Wes's love for the gunsmith's daughter is expressed through dialogue based on a series of *double entendres*, relating the making, fitting and cleaning of rifles to the sexual act. This dialogue leads up to a concentrated image that is typical Fuller. The camera tracks up the rifling of the gun-barrel towards a close-up of the girl framed in its mouth, and then there is a mix through to their first kiss.

When Griff meets Jessica Drummond for the first time she is seated at the head of a huge table with twenty men on each side. The camera cranes along the table passing over the men to come to rest on Jessica. This scene doesn't only stress the strength of Jessica's sex drives and her domination of men. The dialogue makes it clear that these men run the territories on her behalf; there are politicians and lawyers among them;

Forty Guns: the Bonnell brothers – Barry Sullivan (Griff), Gene Barry (Wes), John Ericson (Brock); Griff shoots Jessica

her sexual domination is firmly linked to her political and financial power. Put another way, her political and financial power are seen as an expression of frustrated sexual desire. Similarly, the wilting flowers and the hair-cream stored in the refrigerator link the sexual inadequacy of General Cummings in Walsh's *The Naked and the Dead* with the cold totalitarianism of the Army high command, as opposed to the anarchistic animal vitality of Sergeant Croft. A linking of high finance, Fascist violence and sexual frustration is one of the dominating themes of Penn's *The Chase*. Fuller stresses the connection later in *Forty Guns* when Jessica replies to Logan's declaration of love by writing him out a cheque. That Jessica's desires are unsatisfied is made clear in the continuation of this scene at the table. She dismisses the men and asks Griff to join her in a drink. She comes straight to the point, saying: 'I'm not interested in you, it's your trade I'm interested in, let me see it.' Griff hands her his gun and she fondles it in a directly sexual way. Griff is not uninterested. As he leaves he says in an aside to Logan: 'That's good whisky, you should try some.' The clash of sexual drives that will lead to the inevitable tragedy of the movie is established. What Raymond Williams wrote of Strindberg in *Modern Tragedy* applies in certain measure to all Fuller's relationships, but above all to that between Griff and Jessica. 'Relationship is then by definition destructive: not only because isolated beings cannot combine, can only collide and damage each other; but also because the brief experiences of physical union, whether in sexual love or in infancy, are inevitably destructive, breaking or threatening the isolation which is all that is known of individuality.' Characteristically, Fuller links this relationship to war. As Jessica says to Griff: 'What's happening to us is like war, easy to start and hard to stop.'

It is from the essentially destructive nature of this central relationship that the pervasive violence of *Forty Guns* emanates. Ironically, both Griff and Jessica try to contain the violence; Jessica takes away Brock's guns and tells Logan,

'Murder never solved anything.' Griff's attempts to avoid violence are dramatized in his relationship with his brother Chico. He is always trying to get Chico out of town, but at the same time it is he who gives Chico a gun. 'You brought me up to handle a gun.' In this same scene Griff points out to Chico that the frontier is finished and that he, like the Roman gladiators, is an outdated freak. Here Fuller breaks the conventions of the Western genre by making Griff share his own awareness of the problems of contemporary America. He presents violence as that society's tragic flaw.

Fuller has said that he is not really interested in Westerns. Of Jesse James he said: 'If I meet him in another life I'll stomp him, he was a phoney, the best female impersonator in Kansas.' In *Forty Guns* he is also concerned with stripping away the myth of the West, the fake heroics and chivalry. Griff, like the real Wyatt Earp, never goes out to face anyone in a gunfight unless covered by someone else with a rifle. When he shoots down Jessica, one of the central myths of the frontier – the noble cowboy knight defending the honour of American womanhood – crumbles before our eyes. *Forty Guns* is probably the supreme anti-Western, true precursor of *The Chase*, the central modern anti-Western. The frontier is the place where the poison of violence enters the bloodstream of America. The beautiful dream of the pioneer farmer, the dream Griff has for Chico, is seen to be as impossible as the dream of marriage and children. In Fordian terms the wilderness overruns the garden, and Chico comes into his birthright of violence. He comes to manhood, not through a woman, but through a gun. When he saves Griff's life by shooting one of Jessica's gunmen in the back, he is exultant. Then he sees Griff glaring up at him. 'Now what have I done?' he protests. 'You've killed a man', Griff replies. And so whether on the side of disorder like Brock or order like Chico, the children of America are seen to be irrevocably formed by violence, warped by that failure of love that lies at the heart of individualism and turns us all into freaks.

Griff is a father figure to both Chico and Brock. He fails them both because, like Zack, he was not prepared to break until it was too late. The Western hero is seen as flawed by the very strength of his individuality. He is death-orientated. By shooting Jessica, Griff tries to destroy within himself the evidence of passion, of love, just as Zack does by shooting the North Korean Major. By trying to preserve his individuality inviolate he destroys woman, the symbol of sanity and love. He denies with his bullets the possibility of transcending self.

4: Fuller, Society and National Identity

The problem of violence in American society examined in *Forty Guns* is also the central theme of Anthony Mann's movies. But Mann lays bare the violence within his heroes by removing them from a civilized social context and placing them in a frontier wilderness to face evil alone and unprotected. Movies like *Man of the West* are about Christ in the Wilderness being tempted and falling; they emphasize the advantages of, and indeed necessity for, the restraints of society. The fall back into violence of Mann's hero is seen as temporary; there is always a civilized haven to which he can return. In fact it is in defence of such civilization that the violence is seen as regrettably but occasionally necessary. But for Fuller's characters no such escape is possible; civilization and society are seen as violence in another form.

It is in his view of social organization that Fuller parts company decisively with Hobbes who believed that man was essentially rational and that he would, therefore, agree to succumb willingly to higher authority in order to escape from a permanent state of war. But Fuller believes that irrationality is as basic to man as rationality, and that social organization will always tend to produce further conflict by attempting to frustrate man's deepest drives. Thus just as passionate love and marriage are seen to be in conflict, so too are the individual and society. Indeed, these two concepts are often precisely linked: Cuddles's desire to marry Tolly and her co-operation with Driscoll, the Federal Commissioner, are both aspects of her social urge; Brent's marriage to Helga is symbolic on a personal level of America's attempt to create democracy in occupied Germany. In *The Naked Kiss* it is Grant, society's paragon, who offers Kelly marriage, and the corruptness of that offer is a measure of society's corruptness.

In general, social forms are seen as a fraud, another aspect of the all-pervasive treachery: 'I don't like politics.' In *Forty Guns* the legal system is presented in Brock's trial as a corrupt farce; in *House of Bamboo* and *Underworld USA* the law and crime are seen as basically identical organizations, two armies in conflict; as usual the protagonist is caught between the lines. In *House of Bamboo* the US Army is involved on one side and, on the other, Sandy's gang is run on military lines and made up of 'ex-GIs, fine looking ex-GIs to mix with the the politest people in the politest nation in the world'. Before an operation they are briefed with maps and reconnaissance photographs. During it, they wear uniforms, carry stolen Army weapons, and maintain ruthless military discipline, leaving no wounded on the battlefield. Each side infiltrates the other with a double agent, and Sandy specifically compares his planned treatment of Sergeant Kenner with the way the Army would treat an enemy agent. Both organizations deny individuality and are seen as aspects of creeping totalitarianism. In this context, Sandy's moment of individual human feeling when he saves Kenner's life is seen as a weakness; it is only by ruthlessly suppressing such moments of irrationality that Sandy can preserve his system.

The same comparison is made in *Underworld USA* between the Crime Commission and the Syndicate. Both live in huge inhuman skyscrapers, both use traitors to undermine the other, and both use Tolly to infiltrate the other's organization; both want Tolly to give loyalty to them rather than himself. It's another war. As Connors, the head of the Syndicate, tells his chief lieutenants: 'There'll always be

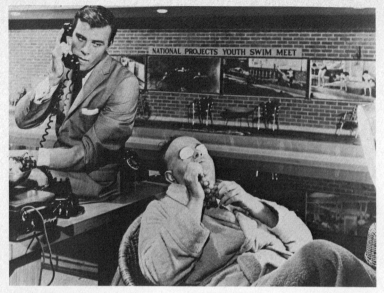
'We'll win the war, we always have': Richard Rust (Gus) and Robert Emhardt (Connors) in *Underworld USA*

people like Driscoll, there'll always be people like us. As long as we keep the books and subscribe to charities we'll win the war, we always have.' When Driscoll briefs his Commission he compares the Syndicate's structure to that of an army. Just as Kenner in *House of Bamboo* has to act like a gangster, in fact *become* a gangster to defeat Sandy, so Driscoll is quite prepared to rub out the gang leaders without the semblance of a trial.

In *Underworld USA* Fuller deals directly with the creeping totalitarianism represented by the corporations and the FBI. Here the presentation of crime recalls the end of Boetticher's *Rise and Fall of Legs Diamond*, where Legs Diamond's individualism is made to appear anachronistic in the modern world of the criminal boardroom, of gangsters in grey flannel suits. As Victor Perkins has pointed out, this development is presented as an historical fact about the United States: 'When he is twelve years old Tolly . . . sees his father beaten to death by four punks. By the time that he is grown up and ready for revenge three of the punks have become leaders of a vice monopoly. There is no reason why the story should be constructed in this way unless Fuller intended the time lapse to be interpreted historically.' This view is confirmed in *House of Bamboo* by the scene in which Sandy meets Spanier/Kenner for the first time. The dialogue stresses the individual nature of Spanier's criminal activities: 'Who are you working for?' 'Spanier.' 'Who's Spanier?' 'Me.' 'And who else?' 'Eddie.' 'Eddie who?' 'Eddie Spanier.' Sandy is incredulous: 'Where have you been the last twenty years? What museum did you crawl out of?' In modern America crime is big business. National Projects maintains a legitimate business façade from basement to penthouse. It is divided into orderly departments, and its takings are recorded on the latest accounting machines. Like a big corporation the Syndicate demands loyalty and team spirit in return for money. When Tolly agrees to crack Driscoll's safe for Gela he says, 'I'd like a future with your organization, a bit of security', as though he were fresh out of Harvard Business School.

It is significant that the opening murder takes place during a drunken New Year's Eve celebration, and that 'Auld Lang Syne' is used as a musical motif throughout the movie. What Fuller is showing is the underside of that much-celebrated prosperity. It is a matter of historical fact that the majority of the great American fortunes were based on extensively criminal activities. But Fuller does not throw up his hands in horror at crime. He regards the normal respectable attitude to crime as deeply hypocritical, a part of that structure of lies which strangles American society and against which his protagonists are fighting. He sees organized crime as nothing more than a logical extension of the mercenary ethic upon which America is built. He has said that his original project for *Underworld USA* was to make a movie about crime in America today showing that it does indeed pay: 'All the good mothers and fathers in America would come out of the movie and say to their sons, you're not going into medicine or the law or IBM, you're going into crime.' In such a society he doesn't condemn people for being mercenary; indeed his protagonists are almost all mercenaries of a sort; they represent us all. But he refuses to allow this fact to be hidden behind a screen of fake moral categories.

This feeling has grown in Fuller's work until in *The Naked Kiss* American society is seen as deeply corrupt at every level. Griff, the policeman and war hero, is both corrupt and hypocritical; he will enjoy Kelly's favours but won't allow prostitutes to practise in his town. Yet in a short exchange of dialogue he is put on the prostitute's level. Kelly refers to him as a cop, a fact he hasn't revealed. 'Is my badge so obvious?' he says. 'Is mine?' she replies. Just as organized crime and big business are equated in *Underworld USA*, so prostitution and big business are equated in *The Naked Kiss*. The earlier relationship between Griff and Kelly is conveyed entirely in the terms of modern advertising. She masquerades as a saleswoman for Angel Foam Champagne, 'Guarantees complete satisfaction', and gives away pens to satisfied customers. Having made love to Kelly, Griff leaves with a pen stuck in his hat.

Immediately after the titles there is a concentrated Fuller image which sums up this theme. Kelly has left her pimp scrabbling about the floor for his money. The sequence ends with a shot of a desk calendar covered with crumpled dollar bills; the date is the 4th of July, Independence Day. This has a double meaning: the vision of independence embodied in America has been soiled by dependence on money, but it's also the day on which Kelly starts her own journey towards freedom. From this shot, Fuller mixes through to her arrival in Grantville. The desperation of the movie lies in the fact that this personal bid for freedom is doomed; destroyed by the all-pervading corruption of American life. Tolly's life began and ended in a garbage-filled alley. Kelly begins and

Independence day: Kelly and her pimp in the opening sequence of *The Naked Kiss*

ends as a prostitute. This corruption is directly linked – through the character of Grant – to big business and the American establishment. Grantville is a company town and Grant owns the business. He is the town's leading citizen, living in a fine house furnished with busts of his ancestors, but the philanthropy and culture that his money provides are seen as merely a front for the essential crime. The Ford and Rockefeller Foundations cannot hide for ever the essentially life-denying processes of corporate capitalism.

In *House of Bamboo, Underworld USA* and *The Naked Kiss*, these totalitarian organizations are shown to be a direct threat to children. Sandy starts his final gun battle with the police in the midst of a crowded children's playground, the Syndicate are starting to push drugs in the schools, and Gus rubs out Menken's daughter, without any compunction, to stop him squealing. Grant, of course, is a child-molester.

'We know the wheel's fixed, but it's the only wheel in town': the food riot in *Verboten*; the ambush of the supply train in *House of Bamboo*

Children are a symbol of life and hope and by destroying them these organizations join with the forces of death.

Grant returns from Europe with a skull in the form of a drinking cup as a present for his servant. In *The Naked Kiss* Europe is seen as a death symbol, a cultural expression of those old social pressures from which America was to be an escape: 'A black revulsion from Europe, from the old authority of Europe, from kings and bishops and popes.' This theme is central to *The Baron of Arizona*. Reavis's ancient European claims are seen as a threat to the individuality of the settlers in Arizona, his assumption of aristocratic European manners as part of a strategy of deceit and of an unhealthy obsession. The same link is enforced in *The Naked Kiss* where Grant's culture, his love for Beethoven, Byron and Baudelaire, are seen as a mere gloss to underlying depravity. This is a traditional American view of Europe, expressed by Henry James among others; pure, innocent America – depraved, devious, corrupt Europe. In Fuller, as in James, the issue is more complex than that, and in the work of both the energy and will to liberty of the American is seen to contain its own corruption.

In Fuller the idea of ancient cultures as limits to freedom is used to link the internal totalitarian threat to the external. In *Verboten*, post-war Germany is presented as basically corrupt and undemocratic. As the Captain puts it: 'We know the wheel's fixed but it's the only wheel in town.' From the first images we are involved emotionally in the problem – is there a difference between a German and a Nazi? – by Fuller's use of Beethoven's Fifth Symphony to accompany Brent's pursuit of the German sniper. This is not a phoney dilemma. Fuller admires Beethoven as much as he detests the Nazis, but it is the themes of Beethoven and Wagner that accompany Brent's ever-deeper involvement in German politics: '. . . I'm up to my neck in double-crosses in this damn country.' The neo-Nazi Werewolf movement, like Grant, uses a bogus reference to history to legitimize its activities; it is seen as a corrupter of young children, a form of juvenile delinquency.

Like the Syndicate in *Underworld USA* it is a criminal organization operating a black-market network, using military tactics and uniforms. To steal a US Army supply truck, they stick a farm wagon across the road; the same ruse is used by Sandy's gang when they ambush the Army supply train in the opening sequence of *House of Bamboo*.

Just as Sandy's moment of human weakness when he saves Eddie's life is seen as an aberration within a totalitarian system, so the North Korean Major in *Steel Helmet* scoffs at Short Round's love for Zack. The connection between Communism and death is made specific in a scene in *China Gate* in which Major Cham, presented as a highly cultured schoolmaster, shows Lucky Legs his arsenal. It is this which he offers her and her son, in place of America. The offer is linked again to marriage. 'I'll show you why it's logical that you should marry me.' Then, among the gleaming bombs and shells, in another of Fuller's stark caves, Cham proclaims his faith: 'This is my garden, these are my revelations.' It is significant that Cham should want marriage to be a logical decision. Logic in Fuller's world is anti-human; it is linked to death, as when Sandy cradles the head of the dying Griff and intones: 'I'm right, I always am'. It is also linked to systems of command, as when Zack says to the Lieutenant: 'If I was right all the time I would be an officer.'

So Fuller's opposition to totalitarianism is an aspect of the basic dilemma of individualism, the absolute opposition of life and death. 'Everyone has a reason for living and a price for dying.' The Fuller protagonist is always caught in a cross-fire between warring totalitarian organizations. His destiny is tragic. His reasons for living lead, as in the case of Tolly, to death, a price which must always be too high, but which he must always pay. The only question that remains is – how should he die? Fuller's answer, like Hemingway's and Mailer's, is – fighting to preserve his individuality in all its irrationality.

In these terms, to regard *Pickup on South Street* as an anti-Communist tract is absurd. Those who wish, in order to

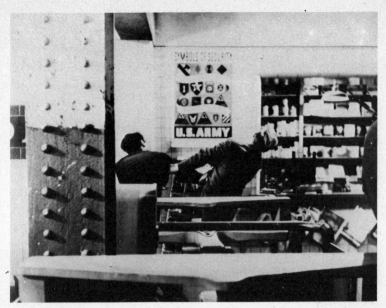

The fight against Communism: *Pickup on South Street*

dismiss his work, to label Fuller as a simple anti-Communist, as a sort of movie McCarthy, pick on the FBI man's line after Candy has agreed to help them get the Commie agent: 'I told you there was a difference between pickpockets and traitors.' But they forget the context in which the line is placed – it is spoken by a man who has been presented as a member of a system seen by Skip and Candy and Moe as absurd, if not hostile. The thick-headed patriotism of the FBI has already been placed by Skip's: 'Are you waving the flag at me?' Anyway, Candy is only co-operating to protect Skip. The true reason for her actions and the feelings embodied by Fuller in the movie are contained in her line to Skip from the hospital bed: 'I'd rather see a live pickpocket than a dead traitor.' I do not wish to deny the presence of anti-Communism in Fuller's work. But it is in many critics' minds such a major blockage to the acceptance of his work that its nature must be accurately defined.

It must be emphasized, however, that Fuller's anti-Communism is far from simple. It is, for a start, part of the dramatic structure. In general, the Communists fulfil two dramatic functions in Fuller's movies. They are often nightmare figures in the minds of the characters, associated directly with mental breakdown. The attack on the temple in *The Steel Helmet* is presented as a part of Zack's breakdown. The charging North Koreans could almost be figments of his deranged imagination. A Russian soldier actually appears in a recurrent nightmare to the Hungarian mercenary in *China Gate* and, of course, it is Communist brain-washing that has helped to send Trent mad in *Shock Corridor*. In these cases Communism has a function similar to that of the murderers of Tolly's father. It is seen as part of a peculiarly neurotic American obsession.

But Communists are also important for the effect they have on the actions of the main characters. They often act as crucial catalysts. Thus, the North Korean Major forces Zack to face up to his emotional blockage; the Communist threat in *Hell and High Water* teaches Adam Jones to accept orders as well as give them. In *Fixed Bayonets* it is the Communist tank that forces Denno finally to overcome his cowardice, and in *Pickup on South Street* it is the Communist agent who forces Skip to admit his love for both Moe and Candy. So here Communism is being used as the Other against which the characters and America define themselves. If Communism wasn't there it would be necessary for America to invent it.

When Lucky Legs comes to see the commander of the French garrison he tells her that he has something important to discuss with her. 'Important to whom?' she immediately retorts. When he tries to enlist her support in an effort to sabotage the Communist arsenal she at first refuses. 'This isn't my war. As far as I'm concerned you and the hammer and sickle boys can fight it out between yourselves.' The

Communism as nightmare: Hari Rhodes (Trent) in *Shock Corridor*

remark is made by the most admirable person in the movie.
Fuller's anti-Communism is one aspect of his dislike of all
systems of authority which try to deny the essential confusions and conflicts of life. His anti-Communism is similar
to Mailer's; and Mailer, we should remember, has been
deeply influenced by Marxism. Fuller has just written *The
Rifle*, a novel about Vietnam, which he hopes to film. In this
book there are sections devoted to South Vietnam, North
Vietnam, America, Russia and China. In the South Vietnamese
section the South Vietnamese are right, in the North
Vietnamese section Ho Chi Minh is right. Nixon, Kosygin
and Mao are also right, in their own sections. As Fuller
explains it, the whole point of the book is to show that they're
all wrong. Fuller is basically an anarchist: 'You cannot force
people to love one another, to think in the same way. You
cannot make them, and I'm delighted. I love confusion, I

117

The New Frontier: Darvi and Widmark in *Hell and High Water*

love conflict, I love argument. If the whole world believed the same thing – imagine a world inhabited only by women or men, it would be terrible. Even if you're right you have no right to impose your way of thinking on me.'

It is ironical that the element of anti-Communism in Fuller's work should be used to dismiss him critically, for it is this very element that attests to the central importance of his work. By handling this theme Fuller has had the courage, unique in American cinema, to confront head on one of the main symptoms of America's struggle to find a national identity. If in one sense all Fuller movies are war movies, in another sense they are all Westerns – the true Westerns of the new frontier. For the concept of the frontier is central to the experience of America. Fiedler in *Love and Death in the American Novel* writes: 'The American writer inhabits a country at once the dream of Europe and a fact of history; he lives on the lost horizon of an endlessly retreating vision of innocence – on the "frontier", which is to say, the margin, where the theory of original goodness and the fact of original sin come face to face.'

The importance of this vision is that it is endlessly retreating. America identifies herself by her headlong flight from Europe. According to Fiedler, to the Renaissance European mind the opening of the West, the discovery of America, did not stand for, but was, a sin, a fall into terrible freedom: 'Ever since, the typical male protagonist of our fiction has been a man on the run, harried into the forests and out to sea, down the river or into combat – anywhere to avoid "civilization", which is to say the confrontation of a man and a woman which leads to the fall of sex, marriage, and responsibility.' The application of this to Fuller's world should by now be obvious. But the true crisis comes when the frontier stops retreating. The fact that the frontier is dead is twice repeated in *Forty Guns*. 'No more towns to break, no more men to break,' as Jessica Drummond puts it. When America's internal expansion has ended, where does the American flee civilization now? He journeys further West; Korea and Vietnam became the new frontier, the gooks and the Vietcong, the new Indians. The US cavalry ride in helicopters now, but they still wear a yellow ribbon. It is no accident that it was Kennedy's new frontiersmen who got the US into Vietnam. I call *The Steel Helmet*, *Fixed Bayonets*, *Hell and High Water* and *China Gate* Westerns, just as Mailer connects Texas and hunting in Alaska, the last true outpost of the Wild West on the North American continent, with American involvement in Vietnam.

The great question facing Americans is – what is an American? The Declaration of Independence laid claim to a new type of country, a New World – its history was the history of Europe, and that was a history it not only wanted to forget but had to forget if it was to forge a new nation out of the pieces of British, French and Spanish culture with which it started. The United States was an artificial creation with a carefully composed written Constitution. You can create a nation overnight, but a sense of national identity takes a long time to build. As man cannot live without some kind of cultural framework, he carries one around like a snail its shell; the early Americans remained in many ways British, French or Spanish and must have thought of themselves as such. The situation grew worse, as wave after wave of slaves and immigrants complicated the racial mix. So those born American could never feel at ease with their national identity, for it was an identity that had to recognize these new immigrants whom the older-established groups found profoundly alien. So what could they reply to the question, what is an American? Their only answer lay in action, hence the significance of the phrase 'unAmerican activities'; it was by building the country that they defined themselves. The American had to live on a perpetual frontier where an American defined himself by comparison with those who weren't American, from Red Indians through Mexicans to Communists. As Mailer put it in *Cannibals and Christians*: '. . . nearly everyone in America is a member of a minority group, alienated from the self by a double sense of identity and so at the mercy of a self which demands action and more action to define the most rudimentary borders of identity'.

We are here at the heart of that movie tradition which has dwelt upon the acts by which the United States has been forged. As a supreme medium for the meaningful deployment of action, the movies are peculiarly suited to make sense of this process of definition undergone by the United States; the attempt to answer the question: 'What is an American?' It is a tradition whose first great work is *Birth of a Nation*. It continues with silent Vidor films like *The Big Parade* and *The Crowd* and sound Vidors like *North West Passage* and *Ruby Gentry*, movies as different as De Mille's *Union Pacific* and Renoir's *The Southerner*. The tradition finds its supreme expression in the work of John Ford – not only the pure Westerns like *My Darling Clementine*, *Fort Apache* or *She*

Wore A Yellow Ribbon, but also the crypto-Westerns, *Young Mr Lincoln*, *The Grapes of Wrath*, *Tobacco Road*. Ford's movies are the culmination of the first phase of the tradition; they are generally optimistic portraits of a dream becoming reality, in which a theory of original goodness still outweighs the fact of original sin. Ford, Vidor and De Mille are of a generation for whom the physical frontier was still a reality, if only just, and as long as that frontier existed the sheer exhilaration of physical progress, of forward movement, compensated for the failures, for all the violence against man and nature that went into the building of America. John Wayne's *The Alamo* was the last movie in this tradition. But as Ford recognizes in *The Man who Shot Liberty Valance* and *Cheyenne Autumn*, two great movies of transition, that era is over. Lawrence noted in *Studies in Classic American Literature*: 'The moment the last nuclei of Red life break up in America then the white men will have to reckon with the full force of the demon of the continent . . . within the present generation the surviving Red Indians are due to merge in the great white swamp. Then the Daimon of America will work overtly, and we shall see real changes.'

Fuller is one of the leaders of a new generation of directors who have faced the Daimon. In *Run of the Arrow* there is a new, darker, more complex tone. It is a movie to put alongside Ray's *The Savage Innocents*, as a true Western of the new frontier. Both are movies about incompatible cultures, but Ray looks at North American civilization through the eyes of the Eskimo. It is with the Eskimo that we feel his sympathy lies, and it is perhaps significant that Ray has in fact deserted America and at the time of writing ceased to make movies. In *Run of the Arrow* the conflicts are internalized within O'Meara, the American. He sympathizes with the Indian way of life and yet he can never be a part of it. For good or ill he is an American and he returns to face what that entails. In the same way Fuller has so far resisted the traps that exile represents for an American movie-maker. Europe destroyed the talents of Anthony Mann, reduced Ray to silence, and Welles almost to silence. It has eaten away at Losey's talents and with Aldrich it was a close run thing – he returned home just in time.

Run of the Arrow opens with a track over the debris of the battlefield. Our noses are rubbed immediately into the results of human conflict. We are reminded of the ruined village at the start of *China Gate*, the field of corpses in *The Steel Helmet*, and the street fighting in the ruined town in *Verboten*. But this time we are in America. This is no escapist fantasy, but a specific moment in history. A glaring red title tells us that this is Palm Sunday, 1865, the last day of the war between the states. A horse picks its way through the debris, an exhausted man slumped in the saddle. He looks like one of the defeated – he is in fact one of the victors. Suddenly a shot rings out and the man falls from his horse. O'Meara walks across a smoke-shrouded stubble field looking round suspiciously, squats over the body and goes through the pockets. Immediately he finds food he stuffs it in his mouth. This recalls Sergeant Zack as he sits among the dead bodies, attending to his immediate bodily needs. We are plunged straight into the Fuller world of suspicion, sudden violence, and the struggle for survival, but this time the Fuller protagonist is put into a specific political environment and his destiny is related directly to the existence of the United States.

From the start Fuller forces the audience to share O'Meara's sense of alienation, and so to live through, with O'Meara, the tensions and confusions that Fuller sees as inherent in being an American. We are told twice in the movie: 'Lee's surrender marked not the death of the South but the birth of the United States.' But the opening images underline the pain of that birth: one American preying on the body of a fellow American like a wild animal. If the nation defines itself in terms of shared experience how can North and South be brought together when one experienced victory and the other defeat? Especially when the United States' image of itself is bound up with success and equates defeat with failure. The psychological scar inflicted on O'Meara can still be seen all over the American South. O'Meara's mother says to her son: 'There is no cure for what ails thee.' But O'Meara retorts, referring to his dead brothers: 'I buried them, you didn't.' For Fuller valid political or moral acts have to come out of personal experience. Merrill asks his unit doctor: 'How do you know what I can live with?' In *Run of the Arrow* we share O'Meara's struggle to find out where he belongs. Like so many Fuller heroes he chooses to become a renegade. Before he goes his friends present him with the bullet with which he failed to kill the US trooper Driscoll, and this last bullet fired in the Civil War, suitably inscribed, he keeps in a pouch hung round his neck. So he goes off, literally carrying his hate with him. Just as the bullet failed to do its job, there is some part of his personality frustrated, unresolved. Like all Fuller heroes he is driven by deep irrational impulses, and there is a typical irony in the remark he addresses to the Indian renegade scout, Walking Coyote: 'I don't have to be anything. I'm a rebel because I choose to be.'

In *The Return of the Vanishing American* Leslie Fiedler examines the way in which American consciousness had defined itself in terms of its relationship to the Indian. He sees this relationship expressed in four basic myths: *Run of the Arrow* combines three of these four. There is first the myth of the runaway male, the original Rip Van Winkle story, which is the rejection of the East Coast and therefore of European social conventions, an assertion of pure anti-social individuality. In the original Van Winkle story the East is represented by a railing wife, a figure corresponding to O'Meara's mother. This rejection of the small-town feminine 'homebody' view of America will be worked out more extensively by Fuller in *The Naked Kiss*, though along with his interest in renegades and outsiders it clearly underlies all his work. 'The enemy of society on the run towards "freedom" is also the pariah in flight from his guilt, the guilt of that very flight' (*Love and Death in the American Novel*).

Then there is the myth of Pocahontas, the Indian maiden who saves the white hero and with whom she returns to civilization. In *Run of the Arrow* O'Meara is saved by Yellow Moccasin, marries her and eventually takes her back to live in the United States. Fuller uses this myth as part of the pattern of contradiction and tension through which he examines his theme. Many people have wondered why Yellow Moccasin saves O'Meara, thus going against her own culture and violating the Run, a crime for which Driscoll will later be executed. In the movie as it stands there is no explanation, though I think one can sense what was originally explained, according to Fuller, in a scene that was never shot: that Yellow Moccasin, like Walking Coyote, is also a mirror image of O'Meara – she too is attracted by a different culture. Perhaps, like Lucky Legs, she wants her orphan ward, Silent Tongue, to be brought up as an American. Whatever the reason her contribution to the tone on which the movie ends is paradoxical. It is she who finally persuades O'Meara that it is impossible to renounce one's nationality, and yet she then leaves with him to go back to the United States in the Pocahontas tradition. The image of their return is combined with a reiteration of the phrase about Lee's surrender and with a title that states: 'The end of this story will be written by you.' The Civil War was largely fought on the issue of colour, an issue that remains central to the nature of the United States. In these terms Yellow Moccasin and the other Indians are coloured. The end of *Run of the Arrow* seems to imply that only when O'Meara has accepted the Indians as other and equal can he be reintegrated into the United States. The superiority of the United States is that it can and must include everyone.

The third archetypal myth embodied in *Run of the Arrow* is the myth of the good companion in the wilderness; Fenimore Cooper's Natty Bumppo and Chingachgook. As Fiedler writes in *The Return of the Vanishing American*: '. . . the essential myth of the West and, therefore, of ourselves, is not

Run of the Arrow: the marriage of O'Meara and Yellow Moccasin; Walking Coyote (Jay C. Flippen) and Crazy Wolf (H. M. Wynant) on the Run

the myth of John Smith and Pocahontas, no matter how we invert or distort it, but the myth of Natty Bumppo and Chingachgook. Here is, for us – for better or for worse, and apparently forever – the heart of the matter: the confrontation in the wilderness of the White European refugee from civilization and the "stern imperturbable warrior".' Fuller uses several variations of this relationship. The first Indian O'Meara meets is Walking Coyote. He is the exact reverse of O'Meara, a renegade returning to his own culture to die. It is he who first fires O'Meara's enthusiasm for Indian culture and teaches him some Sioux, but by his very existence, his final affirmation of the Indian rather than the white way of life, he casts doubt upon the possibility of O'Meara's endeavour.

Such mirror images run right through the film and have the effect of breaking down the differences between the two cultures. The sympathetic Indian chief Red Cloud is paralleled by Captain Clark, who insists against all provocations on co-operating with the Indians. The psychotically violent rebelliousness of Crazy Wolf, who wants to kill all white men, is paralleled in Driscoll who believes that the only good Indian is a dead Indian. Just before the first Run of the arrow, Walking Coyote claims that things among Indians are not what they used to be – no respect for their elders, etc., i.e. the troubles that affect white society also affect Indians. Red Cloud discusses religion with O'Meara and decides that they worship the same God by different names. The saving of O'Meara by Yellow Moccasin, an expression of interracial sympathy, is paralleled by the trooper saving Silent Tongue from the quicksand at the cost of his life. The first such act is followed by the sequence in which O'Meara sweats out his fever, his delirium in clouds of steam the image of a nightmare. It is not the physical fever which is being cured but the scourge of hate: 'There is no cure for what ails thee.' You can only combat active hate with active love. The saving of Silent Tongue is followed by the scene in which Captain Clark tells O'Meara the story of Nolan, the traitor who was never allowed to return to the

United States and lived and died at sea, a permanent exile. It is during this scene that Clark first makes the remark about Lee's surrender being not the death of the South but the birth of the United States. O'Meara is by no means convinced, but we feel that this is the next step in his developing consciousness of himself as an American.

But this movement towards reintegration is constantly threatened; no situation is ever stable in a Fuller movie, and no goal is reached without effort. The reconciliation between European and Indian represented by Clark and Red Cloud is threatened by the haters, Crazy Wolf and Driscoll, and Clark himself is killed. O'Meara, like so many Fuller protagonists, is caught between two warring sides and he will not come to face his nationality until another cycle of violence has worked itself out. And it works itself out, just as the Civil War did, by O'Meara shooting Driscoll. This scene can be read as O'Meara recognizing his brotherhood with Driscoll, a fellow American, and, by sparing his suffering, finally rejecting the Sioux. But to me the scene has a much richer meaning, especially in the total context of Fuller's work. In Fuller's movies it is invariably and paradoxically out of selfishness that the greater good comes, if it comes at all. Up to this moment all O'Meara's actions have a highly personal motivation. Although in my opinion the tone of the film contradicts this, Fuller himself says that at the end O'Meara has learnt nothing and forgotten nothing, he is still full of hatred; and certainly the last image represents the United States as a burnt-out fort and a wagon-load of wounded men, an image almost as bleak as the one with which the movie began. *Run of the Arrow* is about an America that is continually fighting wars to end wars, a country frustrated because its great military and economic power can never solve the problems that face it. *Verboten* examines this dilemma in a specifically modern context, asking why Germany, Europe, the world, are not more grateful to America. George Steiner, in a review of Chomsky's *American Power and the New Mandarins*, wrote:

'Underlying his passionate, often moving indictment is the nearly religious conviction, in itself so American, that America must be different, that the savageries and follies committed by other nations (in Biafra, in Tibet, in Prague) are somehow irrelevant. For America to act as all other major powers have throughout history is, to Chomsky and the New Left, a kind of metaphysical foulness, a betrayal of unique ideas and possibilities.' O'Meara's hate is a rejection of just these savageries and follies, a reaction to this betrayal. When O'Meara shoots Driscoll he is finishing a job, or rather he is trying to grasp at an absolute free of all compromise. By finally firing that last shot of the Civil War he has purged his unsatisfied hate, but by having to purge it he shows that at heart he is unreconciled. He sees Driscoll not as a brother but an enemy. Just as Walking Coyote calls for the Run, not to save O'Meara, but to save himself from hanging – he believes that if he is hung his soul will die – so O'Meara sees the Indians taking away his chance of revenge. Once his personal vendetta is over he has no further use for the Indians.

It is part of the richness of Fuller's work that this ending in no way contradicts the Pocahontas ending of racial harmony and inclusiveness. His view of the world, and here of the United States, incorporates these contradictions. We are unified as much by our mutual hates as our mutual loves, but these are individual rather than racial matters. Mailer wrote in 'The White Negro': 'What is consequent therefore is the divorce of man from his values, the liberation of the self from the Super-Ego of society . . . to open the limits of the possible for oneself, for oneself alone, because that is one's need. Yet in widening the arena of the possible one widens it reciprocally for others as well, so that the nihilistic fulfilment of each man's desire contains its antithesis of human co-operation.'

Although *Run of the Arrow* is the most obvious example of Fuller's treatment of the theme of national identity, he examines the dialectic of allegiance to self and allegiance to country in most of the other works too. Fuller is certainly no simple patriot: when the FBI in *Pickup on South Street* try to persuade Skip to help them combat Communism, his retort ('Are you waving the flag at me?') represents Fuller's own attitude. 'The majority of people are prepared to fight but it isn't really for their country or for an ideal but because they value their lives. I can't stand patriots. Lincoln once said something remarkable – "Patriotism is the last resort of a scoundrel".' In *China Gate*, the 'Marseillaise', one of the great patriotic songs, is played by drunken savages who don't understand it and used as cover by an infiltrating band of mercenaries who are indeed fighting for France; but only one of them is French and among their motives patriotism is notable by its absence.

In *Run of the Arrow* the final test question put to O'Meara by Red Cloud is: 'Would you be prepared to kill your own countrymen if they were fighting the Sioux?' The willingness to die for one's country is usually seen as the ultimate test of patriotism. So it is hardly surprising if Fuller first examines the theme of national allegiance in a war context; in fact he extends to nationality the principle of *I Shot Jesse James*, where at the end Bob Ford challenges Kelley with: 'You don't love her enough to kill for her.' Not die for her, notice. In a world where the fear of death is the absolute motive, to die for one's country is stupid. Dying for one's country is seen as merely an unfortunate by-product of one's willingness to kill for one's country. At the end of *The Steel Helmet* the ex-conscientious objector who was going to be a priest leaps behind a machine-gun yelling: 'If you want to live in a house you've got to be prepared to defend it.' What Fuller never does is pretend that this defence is easy; much of the contempt small-town America incurs in *The Naked Kiss* is because its inhabitants want all the advantages of protection without paying its price. The little white-haired lady keeps a room as a shrine to her dead fiancé, with his uniforms on a dressmaker's dummy, an unhealthy romanticizing of war to set against the central fact in *The Naked Kiss*, that the Korean War hero is a

'A medal is two-faced': Kelly with the dress-maker's dummy in *The Naked Kiss*

pervert. As Fuller himself says: 'A medal is two-faced.' Significantly, the conscientious objector in *The Steel Helmet* is treated with respect by Zack. He had his reasons and he went all the way for them. It is a hypocritical refusal to dirty one's hands that Fuller's movies condemn.

The problem of national identity is complicated in the United States by the central fact of race. The US is, like Lucky Legs, 'a little of everything and a lot of nothing'. In *The Steel Helmet* a North Korean cannot understand why the Negro and the Nisei, a Japanese American, should want to fight for a country that ill-treats them. This is a question that fascinates Fuller too, particularly in relation to the Nisei. In *The Steel Helmet* Sergeant Tanaka replies that their ill-treatment in America is their personal affair and they just don't like outsiders coming in on their fight. And Fuller leaves it at that. In *The Crimson Kimono* he handles the theme at greater length: the connection between this crime thriller and the war films is quite explicit. Charlie Bancroft and Joe Kajaku, one a Caucasian and the other a Nisei, are now Los Angeles detectives who share a flat. But their close friendship developed out of their Korean War experiences, when one saved the other's life. Charlie says, 'I'm walking around with a pint of Joe's blood.' This picks up the theme of blood transfusion as a symbol of basic human unity already used in *The Steel Helmet* when the North Korean is given a transfusion; we remember also that Tolly begins and ends his odyssey beneath a blood donor poster. The connection of *The Crimson Kimono* to the war movies is further underlined by a scene which in terms of plot is completely superfluous. In front of the Nisei war memorial in a Los Angeles cemetery, Fuller shows us the citations from Eisenhower and Ridgway to Nisei gallantry.

In this movie Fuller demonstrates the instability of national identity. The relationship between Charlie and Joe, cemented by war and symbolic of the US, is destroyed by the stresses of peace. As always in Fuller, the destructive force is internal and personal. *The Crimson Kimono* presents a world of cultural integration, reflecting the close friendship between Charlie and Joe. Chris is interested in Japanese art, the stripper Sugar Torch is going to put on a Japanese act, the murderess Roma Wilson is an expert on Japanese dolls and hairstyles, her lover Hansel was advising Sugar Torch on her act. Charlie has become a *kendo* champion, and both he and Joe subdue a giant Korean by using karate. The Nisei, on the other hand, wear American clothes, are unwilling or even unable to speak Japanese, and Joe finds talk of the old country a tiresome bore. Even a Japanese nun appears at one point.

This racial harmony contrasts with the violent disharmony of society which the thriller story presents. The movie opens with a violent murder and ends with the murderess being shot as she tries to escape. Chris, a vital witness, is almost murdered; Charlie and Joe, as policemen, are less integrated into society than the Nisei. They are typical Fuller outsiders. Chris remarks to Charlie: 'You don't look like a cop.' It is meant as a compliment. When Charlie bursts into an apartment block, which a stool pigeon has indicated as the murderer's hideout, he is greeted by the inhabitants with foul-mouthed

Nisei and the theme of national identity: Richard Loo (Sgt. Tanaka) in *The Steel Helmet*; Joe with the Nisei who can't speak Japanese (*The Crimson Kimono*); and the Kendo bout in the same film

hostility rather than co-operation. Charlie and Joe live in a world constantly threatened by violence. Fuller cuts straight from a love scene between Charlie and Chris to the violent karate fight with the Korean, and from a love scene between Joe and Chris straight to Charlie bursting into the apartment block.

In *The Crimson Kimono* racial tensions are created by the eruption of personal feelings, not vice versa. Charlie falls in love with Chris, but Chris falls for Joe, and her feelings are reciprocated. Joe tells Charlie he interprets the look of hate as racial, when, as Charlie puts it, it was 'normal healthy jealous hate'. In the same way Joe sees racial obstacles to his relationship with Chris that just aren't there. This misreading of the situation is mirrored in Roma Wilson's motive for murder: she had killed Sugar Torch because she thought Hansel her lover found the stripper more attractive than her. Her fears are unfounded, just as Joe's are. As she says: 'It was all in my mind.' Her fears lead to murder; Joe's lead to attempted murder when, in the *kendo* bout, he breaks all the rules and really tries to kill Charlie. It is significant that Joe's feelings of racial persecution lead him to reject his own culture, i.e. the rules of *kendo*, whereas Charlie, the white man, obeys the rules. Ironically, he is at that moment more Japanese than Joe. Fuller's cinema breaks down ideologies and categories to go back again and again to individual conflicts and confusions. Racial feeling is an alibi, a convenient excuse for not dealing with personal problems on a personal level; it is dangerous because like other ideologies of hate, Nazism and Communism, it is a way of avoiding rather than facing the truth. And so *The Crimson Kimono* looks forward to one of the images of madness in *Shock Corridor*: a Negro dressed in a white Ku Klux Klan sheet, ranting anti-black slogans and leading a lynch mob in pursuit of another Negro.

5: Fuller, Energy and Madness

'I also like that Eisenstein film, whose title I've forgotten, with that lovely scene of grass bending to the right under the force of the wind, in which the movement of the galloping horsemen changes the direction from right to left. It was a duel between the forces of nature and the horsemen. I love it.' (Fuller)

Here Fuller might almost be describing the opening sequence of his own *Forty Guns*, an extraordinary achievement to come out of Hollywood, for it is really the ultimate underground film, an almost totally abstract display of clashing energies. *Forty Guns* confirms the hip nature of Fuller's visual language and of his concept of character. Mailer wrote in 'The White Negro': 'What makes hip a special language is that it cannot really be taught. If one shares none of the experiences of elation and exhaustion which it is equipped to describe, then it seems merely arch or vulgar or irritating. It is a pictorial language, but pictorial like non-objective art, imbued with the dialectic of small but intense change, a language for the microcosm, in this case man. For it takes the immediate experience of any passing man and magnifies the dynamic of his movements, not specifically but abstractly, so that he is seen more as a vector in a network of forces than as a static character in a crystallized field.' Experiences of exhaustion are particularly common in Fuller's movies: the soldiers throughout the trek in *Merrill's Marauders*; the survivors at the end of *The Steel Helmet* slumped against a pillar in the temple; the crew of the submarine in *Hell and High Water* prostrate from heat and lack of oxygen; Moe lying on her bed just before she is killed; O'Meara at the end of the Run. Fuller sees the process of living very directly in terms of the expenditure of physical energy.

Hobbes wrote that 'there is no such thing as perpetual tranquillity of mind while we live here, because life itself is but motion and can never be without desire, or without fear, no more than without sense', and again, 'there can be no contentment but in proceeding'. One of the glories of the American cinema has been the depiction and celebration of human energy.

From the moment of its discovery the New World was a symbol for the breaking of constraints, for limitless possibilities. It was the visible, physical proof that the maddest journeys would reach a goal, that forward motion would receive its reward. The irony that the world, once circumnavigated, would become even more definitely finite than the Old Known World, was for the moment forgotten. The voyages of discovery seemed to break a dam and release the pent-up energies of Europe.

The United States has made much of its virtue as a non-colonial power and has lectured the old European powers on the evils of their imperialist ways. But in fact conquest and domination have been a constant theme of American history, the very *raison d'être* of a dynamic, expanding society. The successive waves of European settlers pushed back both nature and the Indians. They navigated the great rivers, crossed the mountains, cut down the forests and ploughed the plains. First came the trappers and Indian fighters, then the wagon trains with the ranchers, sod-busters and miners. Then the railroad, and industrial expansion. From East and West they pushed into the interior, grabbing what they could get. Not content with their own vast country they crossed the Rio Grande and stole Texas from Mexico by force of arms. It was the expansionist forces in the United States that started the Civil War. The North didn't really fight the South on moral grounds. It was, rather, a case of a dynamic, rapidly industrializing society confronting a conservative, static society which clung to the old unexpansive ways of Europe. The Yankees came, not to liberate slaves, but to exploit an

135

underdeveloped country. It was the carpet-bagger, not Lincoln, who won the Civil War.

This process of expansion became an accelerating chain reaction. Modern industrial economies cannot stand still. Just as Britain, the world's first great industrial power, had to have an Empire as a market, so too did the United States. In spite of her isolationist instincts and her suspicion of the Old World, this young nation found herself with awful suddenness the world's dominant industrial and (therefore) military power. In such a society, which remains a permanent pioneer society, now plunging out into the frontiers of space, the very act of forward motion, of just doing something, becomes a value in itself. The society's survival depended on driving wagons, fording streams, building houses and factories and railroads, in a much more direct way than in more static European societies. Even today travellers are surprised at the speed with which buildings are torn down and rebuilt in a process of constant expenditure of energy.

At first the movies, like the society they mirrored, didn't question the value of this constant expenditure of energy. They celebrated it for itself. They didn't ask where they were going, they just enjoyed the ride. King Vidor, hauling his boats up the hill in *North West Passage*, Hawks with his cattle drive in *Red River*, John Ford heaving his wagons over the mountain range in *Wagonmaster*; in these movies energy is valued as purely creative. Now the dream has gone sour in the American cinema as it has in American society; only Hawks has maintained his faith in virile energy by severely limiting its scope, so that to compare the ending of *Red River* with the real Fuller ending to *Forty Guns* is to see the extent of the shift in the mood of American movies. There is a false ending to *Forty Guns* in which Jessica Drummond survives, but Fuller meant her to die. The whole logic of the film leads up to the moment at which the hero is forced to kill the woman he loves, or (more important in Fuller's terms) likes and respects. The logic of *Red River* leads up to a death which Hawks could not face. As he said: 'It frustrates me to start killing people off for no reason at all.' Hawks dodges the tragedy inherent in a clash of great individual energies; Fuller rushes towards that tragedy. Indeed, on his own admission, the death scene was the inspiration for the whole film.

The American cinema has begun to count the cost of the energy it once celebrated. Vidor in *Duel in the Sun* and *Ruby Gentry* shows the energy as purely destructive, Ford in *Cheyenne Autumn* shows the genocide caused by the energy depicted before in *Wagonmaster*. But a new generation of American directors has examined the contradictions and the tensions between these two views of energy. In *The Far Country* or *The Man From Laramie* Anthony Mann shows the struggle between destructive and creative energy in society and within the individual. James Stewart is forced against his will to resort to violence, to use destructive energy in defence of the creative. Welles in all his work examines the way in which the energy becomes corrupted: the exciting young idealist Kane becomes the solitary, ageing power-maniac; Quinlan is pulled ever deeper into the mire by his success as a detective. In Kazan and Ray the energy becomes pure neurosis: Kowalski in *A Streetcar Named Desire*, James Dean throwing the ice out of the ice-house in *East of Eden*, the chicken run in Ray's *Rebel Without A Cause*. To see the change in the attitudes to energy, compare Wayne as the typical Hawks or Ford protagonist with Brando and Dean.

Fuller manages to contain these contradictions within one work. He celebrates energy as the ultimate truth because 'life itself is but motion', and indeed he celebrates it all the more because it is doomed, useless energy. It is man's attempt to shun death, but death always wins. The mercenary in *China Gate*: 'This is the life for me but I have to die to live it'; Zack to the North Korean: 'If you die, I'll kill you'; Moe in *Pickup on South Street*: 'If I was buried in Potter's Field it would just about kill me.' The pessimism of Fuller's view is shown by Moe, the character for whom he clearly has great

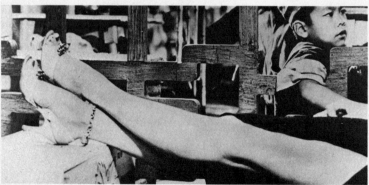

Feet: 'Just put one foot in front of the other' (*Merrill's Marauders*); Lucky Legs

tenderness and respect, whose whole reason for living is to save enough for a decent burial.

Fuller's energy-images are feet. Luc Moullet drew attention, in *Cahiers*, to Fuller's obsession with feet; Fuller laughed and sent him a big rubber foot. But the fact remains that feet play an important role in Fuller's cinema, perhaps because he was an infantryman. As Rock says in *Fixed Bayonets*: 'There are only three things you have to worry about, your rifle and your two feet.' This is shortly followed by the sequence in which the soldiers massage each other's feet to avoid frostbite. Rock finds that one foot is numb, and the sequence ends with a close-up of him pounding his bare feet on the ground to get the circulation going, a symbol of his will to survive. Later in the film Denno walks through the minefield to save his wounded sergeant – the close-up of his boots feeling their way through the snow, in danger of blowing him up every time he puts them down, not only involve the audience in the tension of the scene, but also vividly suggest the willpower he is exerting. It is significant that this willpower is self-contained, because in the film it is useless. The sergeant is dead when he gets him back.

Merrill's Marauders is constructed round the principle of pure energy. When the unit's doctor tells Merrill his men cannot go on because they are suffering from AOE – accumulation of everything – Merrill replies: 'Nothing to it, just put one foot in front of the other.' The characters keep going on a will to survive which, given the evidence, is totally irrational. Merrill's marauders, in spite of putting one foot in front of the other, end up with Merrill himself dead, face down in a puddle, surrounded by a few badly wounded survivors, and they haven't even attained their objective. Part of Fuller's implied criticism of war is that it should cause so much energy to go to waste.

I don't think, as Victor Perkins suggests, that Fuller is trying to equate physical with moral stamina. Fuller is using physical energy or stamina as a symbol for the irrational drives that

139

motivate man. So in *Run of the Arrow* the images of O'Meara's bleeding feet tearing through the stones and the thorns become a symbol of the urgency of his desire to get away from the United States, a desire that must inevitably be frustrated, like his desire to escape from Crazy Wolf. (Walking Coyote has told him that no one has ever survived the Run.)

Fuller's heroes face life with a sort of doomed defiance. They are permanent embodiments of powerful frustrations, symbolized by Tolly Devlin's clenched fist in *Underworld USA*. Tolly's energy is totally obsessional, his whole life is devoted to avenging his father's death personally, with, as always in Fuller, the emphasis on the personal. His father's murder is presented as a play of huge nightmare shadows on the wall. His fists twist the sheet in a nightmare as he lies in bed in the reformatory; then Fuller dissolves through to his hand cracking a safe. He becomes a criminal, goes to prison, voluntarily stunts his own personality in order to fulfil his deepest need. Death is the inevitable end. As with Bob Ford in *I Shot Jesse James*, we feel the death is a suicide, voluntarily sought, for once his revenge is fulfilled he has no reason for living. Moreover, in attaining his aim he has rejected all forms of social integration; as a young boy he refused to fink, to give information to the police which might have helped them to get his father's murderers. He rejects the love and advice of Sandy, his mother substitute. Sandy is revolted by his plan of revenge, and reacts like O'Meara's mother in *Run of the Arrow*, telling him: 'You're sick.' He rejects Cuddles's love, and when she tells Tolly she wants to marry him: 'We've got a right to climb out of the sewer and live like other people', he replies: 'Marry? Marry you?'

These refusals differentiate *Underworld USA* clearly from the film to which it owes the greatest debt, *The Big Heat*. Lang ends his film on a note of social integration with Dave Bannion back in the police force. Both films have a dynamic style, the editing mirroring the driving energy of the two protagonists, but in Fuller's movie the style is completely identified with Tolly. The tracks and shock cuts and rapid dissolves make *Underworld USA* one swift punch, to end in that close-up of a bunched fist. Lang's editing style is more objective and presents a pattern of forces wider than the hero's destiny: Bannion becomes involved in corruption because he is doing his job. It pre-exists him, it is an outside force. He is later forced to leave the police in order to revenge himself, but only because the police are corrupt and will not help him. He accepts help willingly, from anyone who will give it; indeed Lang gives a picture of solidarity, of forces for good always present, only waiting for a focus or leader. So Bannion's personal energies are channelled to social ends, and the fulfilment of his personal revenge is seen as an instrument for cleansing society. Once revenge is accomplished normal life can be resumed; Bannion returns happily to a life of routine police work and shared cups of coffee. In *Underworld USA* there is no normal life, no tranquillity of mind, just a system of clashing individual energies.

Fuller says that what he looks for as a principle on which to organize a script is one character going from right to left and another going from left to right – 'I love conflict.' In *Forty Guns* the energy is destructive because of its very force. Griff Bonnell tries to keep his cool throughout – he is not a man for stupid heroics. He advises his friend the Marshal to leave town because his eyes are failing. 'What', the Marshal asks, 'if the doctor can't do anything for my eyes?' 'Then you'll be blind instead of dead.' The first thing Griff and his brother do on hitting town is to take a bath – there are two key bath scenes in the movie, which, especially as the baths are out of doors, present the men both at their most relaxed and at their most vulnerable. The first is interrupted and the second followed by key scenes of violence, stages in Griff's commitment to destructive personal violence. The symbolic act of cleansing oneself is seen as useless, and Griff confronts Brock with a towel still round his neck. This confrontation is presented as a pure clash of energy, one will against another. Griff's progress is seen as a series of close-ups of walking feet, face, then a huge close-up of his eyes, and finally a track-in to a close-up of Brock's unraised gun. But it is Griff's triumph over Brock which will eventually force his energy into paths of pure destruction; he shoots not only Brock, but Jessica as well, whom he loves. For Brock's energy, his reason for living, has not been destroyed; only death can do that. It has been frustrated and will inevitably burst into new and more dangerous channels. Brock represents the forces of anarchy which Griff is trying to control in himself and others. As Griff says later to Chico, his youngest brother, 'Let's not make this a personal fight.' But that is what it inevitably becomes.

The confrontation with Brock is followed by one of Fuller's most dazzling portrayals of the clash of conflicting energies, and also of the conflict between order and anarchy. In one immensely long crane and tracking shot the camera accompanies the Bonnell brothers from their room in the hotel and along the complete length of the main street to the telegraph office. The object of this walk is the sending of a telegram which will get Chico out of town, away from the life of the gunfighter. This walk symbolizes Griff's desire, if only through the person of his brother, for a settled family life on a farm. As they walk up the street Sheriff Logan tries to ingratiate himself: it is only later that we realize that Logan is in love with Jessica and is for his own reasons trying to head Griff off from his fatal confrontation with Jessica. But after the telegram is sent, and still in the same shot, Jessica and her horsemen come pouring into town and sweep past the camera in the opposite direction to the Bonnell brothers' walk. Griff cannot avoid the confrontation which will also implicate Chico, till now unblooded, in another round of violence.

Griff and Jessica represent two different forms of energy. Griff is law and order and the government in Washington, Jessica is capitalist free enterprise. Her speech to Griff describing her life is a little poem on the building of America, on agriculture, industry and politics. Both forms of energy contain within themselves their own flaw: Griff's is based on the gun and Jessica's on financial corruption. She destroys Logan by replying to his declaration of love with a cheque. The fateful dialectic of the film is expressed in two lines of dialogue between Griff and Jessica. Jessica: 'I need a strong man to carry out my orders.' Griff: 'And a weak man to take them.' They are attracted to each other by their mutual recognition of the strength in the other. This dooms their life, for should either succumb to the other's will, the attraction will, by definition, die. Everything leads up to that final confrontation. Because Jessica loves Griff she allows her empire to crumble. Her legal adviser cannot understand why she has done this, but like Logan she is committing suicide. She had previously said to Griff, offering him a job: 'This is the last stop, the frontier is finished, no more towns to break, no more men to break. It's time you started to break.' And Logan has said to her just before his suicide: 'A man can only wait so long, a man has got to do something about what is in his heart or it will break.' Jessica has been broken by Griff. There is nothing left for him but to shoot her, for in Fuller's world the price of survival is not breaking. For Fuller and for America the frontier is never finished.

The mad destructive nature of energy is made clearer in *Shock Corridor* where sheer physical energy is one of the symptoms of madness. Johnny Barrett tries to assault the psychiatrist and has to be dragged from the office. The asylum is characterized by sudden unmotivated outbursts of violent activity: the riot in the canteen, the nymphomaniacs' assault on Johnny Barrett, the attempted lynching of a Negro. And so the whole process of cure is the destruction of energy. The hot baths and electric shock treatment calm the inmates down, the strait-jacket is held before the patients as a constant threat, and at the end Johnny Barrett is reduced to an almost inanimate object. The film ends on the traditional movie clinch, but this time the man is totally unresponsive. The passion that is the driving force of Fuller's heroes has been killed. It

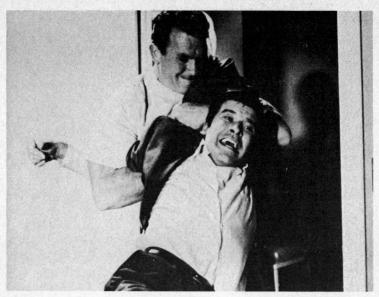

Destructive energy: Barrett dragged from psychiatrist's office; rioting inmates in *Shock Corridor*

has destroyed itself. Absolute rationality meets absolute irrationality in a human vegetable. The price of safety is the destruction of all that makes us living human beings.

This disillusionment with energy is carried further in *The Naked Kiss*. Kelly's treatment of the crippled children recalls Merrill's treatment of his troops. She exerts her willpower to make them triumph over their physical limitations by putting one foot out in front of the other. But this triumph is only a dream. That the children will ever run across the park is an illusion. Only in a sort of insanity can we conquer the limitations of our physical human situation. Norman Mailer describes the same drive towards madness in *The Presidential Papers*: 'Because what we suffer from in America, in that rootless moral wilderness of our expanding life, is the unadmitted terror in each of us that bit by bit, year by year, we are going mad. Very few of us know really where we have

come from and to where we are going, why we do it, and if it is ever worthwhile. For better or for worse we have lost our past, we live in that airless no man's land of the perpetual present, and so suffer doubly as we strike into the future because we have no roots by which to project ourselves forward, or judge our trip.'

As Fuller uses war as an extended metaphor for life, and as he describes war as organized lunacy, it is hardly surprising that insanity should be a major theme of his movies. As we have already seen, his apparently cynical and rational characters are usually in fact doing things for most irrational reasons. As we have also seen, they exist in a world where appearance and reality are so confused that their hold upon reality must inevitably weaken. In a crazy world the most rational stance may in fact be madness, so that insanity faces Fuller's characters not only as a threat but also as a solace, as an escape from the intolerable dilemmas posed by the dialectics of the world in which they roam. For Fuller's characters, because they desire complete liberty, live in a world of perpetual choice. 'For me when I come to a point in a film where there is a cross-roads, the moment where the characters can go in several different directions, where there is a real choice, I am happy.' So these characters must hold, within the confines of their selves, a large number of conflicting possibilities. Moreover, they must make a choice between these possibilities on the basis of evidence which they know from experience to be totally unreliable. What Fuller says of his own experience of war is also true of his characters: 'When you're at the front, you're in a constant state of tension.' This tension comes out of the effort of keeping incompatible forces in equilibrium; for instance, in a war situation the incompatibility between the basic fear of death and the situation in which a soldier is placed. Sergeant Zack's prime aim is survival and yet he has voluntarily signed up again so that he will be in a position where his life is in danger.

Those tensions lead to a crack-up, because they are turned inwards. Society is seen not as a means of fulfilling self but as a frustration of self. So all the conflicts and tensions in the world are piled upon the lone individual consciousness. Joe, in *The Crimson Kimono*, is allowed no social outlet for his problems – Fuller doesn't allow him the luxury of saying, 'I am a helpless victim of the race problem, it is society's fault, not mine.' No, it's his case and he has got to bust it. Ultimately the individual is completely alone, because only he can live within his own consciousness and that consciousness defines his possibilities. As Joe says to Chris: 'You cannot feel for me unless you are me.' And Merrill, to the unit's doctor: 'How do you know what I can live with?' But the corollary of this pure individualism is that no one else can make your choices for you, there is no escape from the dilemma of self. You can put off the moment of choice and Fuller's characters usually do. Denno in *Fixed Bayonets* will go to the length of risking death in the minefield to avoid taking on the responsibilities of command; Skip in *Pickup on South Street* continues to play both ends against the middle until the beating-up of Candy forces him to choose sides; O'Meara tries to become a Sioux rather than face up to the hatreds dividing the United States. But eventually the choice must be faced and it is always seen as a choice that is important because of its effects on the individual. Denno's successful assumption of responsibility is seen as being good, not for the United States, the Army or the war effort, but for him. Any exterior considerations are seen as irrelevant. The self-contained personal nature of the choices is beautifully expressed by the scene in *Fixed Bayonets* in which the frightened medical orderly operates on himself for the removal of a bullet. The camera starts on him and then makes a 360-degree pan round the faces in the cave, returning to the orderly in his moment of triumph as he removes the bullet. The meaning of the act begins and ends with him.

Often the self is unable to stand the tension any longer. One solution, as we have already seen, is suicide. The others are violence and insanity and in Fuller's movies the two are closely linked. In violence the irrational forces driving man are turned outwards and clash head-on with the similar forces in another individual; one of the conflicts experienced by Fuller's characters is that between their own selves and the Other, the world outside which continually circumscribes their freedom of action. Violence is an attempt to resolve that confusion by destroying the Other. In Fuller's world and in American society, violence is, therefore, an inevitable product of a race of masterless men. So war is the denial of other nations, race hatred the denial of other races. The violence with which the Chicago police assaulted the demonstrators at the Democratic Convention was an attempt by the police and the forces they represented to deny the complexity of society, to deny the possibilities of disagreement, not so much in society but within themselves. They were like Zack in *The Steel Helmet* who shoots the North Korean Major, not because he reads out Short Round's prayer, 'Please make Sergeant Zack love me', but because he adds 'What a stupid prayer.' The Major has forced Zack to confront the conflict between his allegiance to another and his allegiance to self. Throughout most of the movie he has agreed with the Major on the stupidity of Short Round's prayer; so when he shoots the Major he is trying to destroy part of himself, trying to deny his own previous cynicism. It is the first sign of his approaching madness.

This pattern of using violence as a form of spiritual suicide, as a way of denying parts of the truth about oneself, recurs in Fuller's movies. Bob Ford, in *I Shot Jesse James*, will not listen when Kelly tells him that Cynthy does not love him. Against a man who is not prepared to accept the truth Kelly is forced to use a shotgun rather than rational argument. Similarly, the violence in *The Baron of Arizona* stems from Reavis's refusal to admit his fraud or make concessions to the settlers. The obsessional nature of his desire for totally individual possession and domination can only be met by an attempt, by bombs or hanging, to destroy that individuality which lies at the centre of the obsession. Communication implies a process of sharing. When this sharing is seen as a violation of individuality, only the actual physical violation of the self remains as a means of communication. Physical coercion becomes the only language that is understood. In *Verboten*, when Bruno tells Brent the truth about Helga, Brent immediately knocks him down. When Brent tells the hungry Germans that America is feeding them, they beat him up. One is reminded of the way the *Star* reacts to the *Globe* in *Park Row*.

After being made to see the truth about the Nazis at Nuremberg, Helga's brother kills the Werewolf leader in a burning railway wagon. This is an attempt to exorcize the guilt of those Nazi war-crimes, to destroy part of Germany and, therefore, part of himself. Nazism is seen as another form of that violence that would attempt to deny the truth, the com-

148

plexity of both society and individual. This is the danger and attraction of Fascism in Fuller's work: as the title *Verboten* implies, Fascism is directly equated with the limitation of personal freedom, but not on the simple political level of the oppressive mechanism of a totalitarian state. Nazism is insanity on the national level. The irrational is so strong that if you deny it and dam it up with excessive social restraints it will burst out in an excessively violent form. Zack denied the love in him for so long that its eventual expression was a burst of machine-gun fire.

This is why war leads to madness. It places an unbearable restraint upon natural human impulses. In *Merrill's Marauders* Chowhound wishes to satisfy the eminently natural desire for food, so he rushes out into the field where the crates of food have been dropped by plane, and is shot down by the surrounding Japanese. In the scene with the dog-tags where Stock has to write letters to the next-of-kin of the dead men, it's made clear that to be a successful soldier he must suppress his natural feelings of sorrow. He must not get too close to his men. Under these circumstances insanity is the natural response. The soldier asks Merrill whether Lemchek got through, and then dies. Merrill asks the medical orderly, 'Who's Lemchek?' 'He's Lemchek', the orderly replies. Later Muley identifies totally with his mule and ends up carrying the animal's load himself, to the point of death from exhaustion. Private Jaszi, one of the mercenaries in *China Gate*, suffers from nightmares in which he sees a Russian soldier standing over him and tries to kill this imaginary adversary. He is similar to Tolly in *Underworld USA*. The murder of Tolly's father is seen by Tolly and by us, the audience, not as a physical killing but as a nightmare of huge shadowy figures. It is a trauma that Tolly can only exorcize through personal violence. The neurotic source of his revenge, which becomes the basis for his whole life, is illustrated by the fist motif. From the very start he refuses to involve society in his quest by not finking to the police. This refusal to fink is a refusal to

149

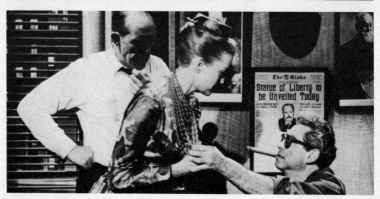

Forms of madness: Chowhound and the food-drop in *Merrill's Marauders*; Tolly in *Underworld USA*; 'I'm saving so we can have a normal life' – Fuller directs Constance Towers in *Shock Corridor*

communicate, to tell the truth. Violence is the only language he can talk. That, as a result, it is a problem that can only be solved by his own death is made clear by the close-up of his clenched fist on which the film ends.

The opening of *Underworld USA* seems to imply some foul primeval curse at the base of American experience. It takes place against the background of party-giving in the alleys behind the speakeasies where New Year's Eve is being celebrated. It seems to lay bare the underbelly of the American dream: while the party goes on unheeding, a terrible crime is being committed, a crime that America can never exorcize. Perhaps it is the denial of the father, of the culture of old Europe, perhaps it is the destruction of the Indians, perhaps it is slavery; perhaps the crime and the curse is individual liberty itself, just as in Oedipus the tragedy comes not from anything he has done but from the awareness that he has done it. If all problems return for their solution to the self, the centre of individual consciousness, they will become, like Tolly's revenge, obsessions. So madness is seen as the inevitable outcome of complete individual liberty.

This theme finds its final expression in *Shock Corridor* where America becomes not a battleground or the frontier or the underworld but a mental asylum. Johnny Barrett is ostensibly trying to solve a murder that has taken place in the mental hospital, just as Tolly is ostensibly tracking down his father's killers. In fact both their aims are projections of their personal obsessions. *Shock Corridor* opens with Barrett being coached to simulate the symptoms of insanity when it is clear – with his ambition to win the Pulitzer Prize at any cost – that he is already insane. This is made clear when his fiancée Cathy tries to dissuade him from his project: 'I'm saving so we can have a normal life.' In the first scene society in the person of a doctor and a newspaper editor is involved in Johnny's insanity. Typically with Fuller, the only sane person is an outsider, a stripper and night-club singer, who, by loving Johnny, has broken out of the obsessive circle of her own individuality. The bitterness of the movie can be measured if you remember Fuller's affectionate tribute to journalism in *Park Row*. Now a newspaper editor and a journalist are essentially implicated in the madness of American society. The fall from grace is summed up at the end of the movie by the head of the mental hospital: 'What a tragedy. An insane mute will win the Pulitzer Prize.' Journalists were seen originally as guardians of the truth, but now they are part of the great conspiracy, part of the totalitarianism of lies that Mailer sees all round him in the mass media. Moreover, the truth is now too hideous to contemplate. It sends those in search of it mad.

That insanity is the ultimate expression of individuality is made clear in a sequence between Barrett and Pagliacci. Pagliacci is conducting imaginary music. We only hear the music during the shots of Pagliacci. During the shots of Barrett we hear only his thoughts. The apparently sane man lives in as self-contained a world as the insane, each totally insulated from the other's experience. This point is further stressed in Barrett's interviews with the three witnesses to the murder. In each case Barrett manages to trigger off a return to sanity. They leave their fantasy identities, but only to return to the obsessive fears that have made them mad. They want in each case to communicate their experiences to Barrett, but Barrett can talk about nothing else but the murder. And so the line between sanity and insanity disappears and we are left only with individuals immured within an obsessively isolated self. That for these isolated individuals violence becomes a substitute form of communication is demonstrated at the end of *Shock Corridor* when Barrett pursues and beats up Wilkes in an orgy of physical violence. He has lost his voice and cannot pass on the secret of Wilkes's guilt in any other way.

The normal stance of suspicion used by the Fuller protagonist as a means of survival becomes in *Shock Corridor* the cause of mental breakdown, and illustrates how close to

152

Cathy

insanity all Fuller's men and women constantly are. It is suspicion of murder which leads Barrett into the asylum in the first place. Once there he becomes obsessively jealous of Cathy. In his dreams Cathy taunts him with her unsatisfied sexuality and her infidelity. This is an imagined infidelity, with which we, the audience – in a typically Fuller manner – are involved, for in the striptease sequences we are made to desire Cathy. She appears to Barrett in his dreams, as she has appeared to us, dressed for her striptease act. To the extent that we desire her it is of us that Barrett is suspicious, but also to the extent that we desire her we share Barrett's frustrations. So we are implicated in the causes of Barrett's insanity and made aware of the possibilities of sharing that insanity.

The world of the insane is not seen as different from the normal world. On the contrary, the mental hospital is a concentrated version of the world of Fuller's other movies. Everyone is playing a false role: Stuart, the defector to Communism, plays a Confederate general; Trent, the only black student at a Southern university, plays the leader of the Ku

153

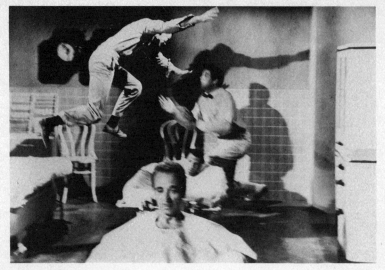

Shock Corridor: Barrett leaps at the murderer

Klux Klan; Boden, the atomic scientist, plays an innocent five-year-old; Barrett, the journalist, plays a madman. The authorities, like society, are either corrupt hypocrites, like Wilkes who appears to be the kindest of the nurses but is in fact a murderer and on the fiddle, or else they devote themselves to containing the impulses of the individual inmates, reducing them by treatment to an inhuman state of calm. Irrationality is so central to Fuller's world that those who devote themselves to making man rational are revealed as absurd: as mad as their patients, locked themselves within their own narrow psychiatric categories. It is a world where bouts of extreme violence may break out at any moment and for the most trivial reasons.

To view *Shock Corridor* is to be reminded of de Sade's comment on the Gothic Novel, quoted by Fiedler in *Love and Death in the American Novel*: ' "It was necessary to call hell to the rescue . . . and to find in the world of nightmare" images adequate to "the history of man in this Iron Age." ' That it is a nightmare version of America is made clear in the persons of Stuart, Trent and Boden, the three witnesses to the murder, for they are also witnesses to America's crimes. Stuart, the son of illiterate sharecroppers in Tennessee, has been brought up to hate rather than to love. After capture in Korea he goes over to the Communists, but having been given something to love in America he rejects Communism and comes home, only to be driven into madness by the rejection of his fellow countrymen. He has lived out the paranoia of the cold war and McCarthyism. Trent has been the first black student of a Southern university. The pressures on him – from his own people, to succeed, and from the whites, hatred – have driven him mad. He is a product of America's racial crime. Boden is a witness to the crimes of technology, especially the dropping of the two atom bombs. His madness is a protest against the perversion of knowledge in the cause of militarism. Like Lear's madness, Johnny Barrett's is the only reasonable response to the horrors he has discovered. In *Shock Corridor* fiction becomes reality, the existential hero defines himself by his acts – by acting madness he becomes mad. Only when his quest is realized is its true nature revealed to him. At the moment in which he discovers the murderer's identity he discovers his own identity, the final expression of his own ambition. He goes mad and retreats completely within himself; only in total isolation can true individual liberty be found, only when he is mute and motionless is Johnny free from other people.

Here at the end of *Shock Corridor* the basic polarity of Fuller's world is contained in the person of Johnny Barrett. He is outwardly a perfect symbol for the forces of the logical rational mind, controlled in his catatonic trance to the point of rigidity. Perfectly adapted to the world in which he finds himself, he has been reduced by social constraints to complete inactivity. But within, the irrational has taken over. The images of his madness are waterfalls and lightning, the forces of untamed nature towards which America has always fled in

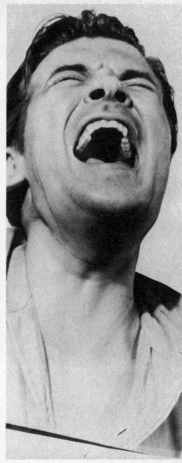

revulsion from the kings and bishops of Europe. Barrett has succumbed to the lure of irresponsibility and insanity symbolized by the two central water images of the American imagination, the river in *Huckleberry Finn* and the ocean in *Moby Dick*.

America is a lunatic asylum

Appendix: Fuller and Godard

Fuller has had a great influence on the modern cinema, but at second hand, through the works of Godard. In his days as a critic, Godard wrote a highly laudatory review of *Forty Guns* in *Cahiers du Cinéma*; in *Breathless*, his first feature, he copies the shot looking down the rifle-barrel. When preparing *Les Carabiniers* he said he wanted to shoot it like a Fuller war movie. In *Pierrot le Fou* Sam Fuller appears, as himself, and briefly states his definition of the cinema, a definition which becomes the motto for Godard's movie. *Made in USA* is dedicated to Nick and Samuel – Nicholas Ray and Samuel Fuller, 'whose pupil I am in terms of sight and sound'. Many Anglo-Saxon critics find it almost perverse that such an intellectual king of the art movies should admire a man they see as just a maker of cheap Hollywood B-features. But Godard's admiration of Fuller is not intellectual slumming or part of an uncritical love of American culture, nor is it marginal. If we admire and respect Godard as possibly the most important contemporary director and certainly the greatest influence on contemporary cinema, then we must also recognize that his debt to Fuller is central to his work.

The Godard hero, the alienated outsider, is an intellectualized version of the Fuller hero. Belmondo in *Breathless* may worship Bogart, and *Made in USA* may be based upon *The Big Sleep*, but Belmondo and Karina are more passionate, irrational and self-destructive characters than Bogart ever played. Of course Godard admires Hawks, but his heroes and heroines share, not Hawks's limited moral certainty, but Fuller's desperate confusion. Dialectic and paradox are as fundamental to Godard's world as to Fuller's. Godard's heroes, like Fuller's, are pickpockets and prostitutes, double agents or men and women fleeing conventional society. Often Godard's debt to Fuller is specific and concrete. Compare, for instance, the washroom scene in *Breathless* with the one in *Pickup on South Street*. Compare the opening shot of *Breathless* – Belmondo peering from behind his newspaper – with similar shots of Widmark in the opening sequence of *Pickup on South Street*. Subor in *Le Petit Soldat* is caught between warring political factions and develops a love relationship in the midst of the battle just as the protagonists of so many Fuller movies do. Subor and Karina play out a typical Fuller drama of loyalty and treachery; they carry on a love-affair under fire just like Skip and Candy, or Brock and Lucky Legs. In *Alphaville* Eddie Constantine offers almost a re-creation of Robert Stack's performance in *House of Bamboo*. Quests and meaningless journeys abound in Godard, during which the protagonists find out as much about themselves as they do about their ostensible goal. *Breathless, Le Petit*

Soldat, *Alphaville*, *Made in USA* and *Pierrot le Fou* all share this very Fullerian structure. The treks through woods and across streams in *Pierrot le Fou* remind one of *Merrill's Marauders*, and the journey ends on a similarly nihilistic image. But Pierrot and the hippies in *Weekend* are also O'Meara trying to flee to a more primitive world to escape the moral dilemmas posed by modern society. The measure of Fuller's strength in comparison to Godard is that O'Meara returns whereas Pierrot commits suicide.

All Godard's men in their relationships with women might reiterate Brent's remark in *Verboten*, 'I couldn't believe you no matter what you tell me. . . .' Belmondo is betrayed by Seberg in *Breathless*, Subor by Karina in *Le Petit Soldat*, Piccoli by Bardot in *Contempt*, Belmondo by Karina in *Pierrot le Fou*. The double-cross is central to Godard's world as it is to Fuller's, and Godard's heroes are, like Fuller's, aware of the emotional booby-traps through which they must thread their way. They are doomed by love. The long love scenes which resemble interrogations in *Breathless*, *Le Petit Soldat*, *Contempt* and *Pierrot le Fou* doom the hero and heroine to misunderstanding just because of those ambiguities of language and appearance that also concern Fuller. Bardot in *Contempt* might well have said to Piccoli, 'You only saw what you wanted to see.' Belmondo's final grimace in *Breathless*, his blue-painted face in *Pierrot le Fou*, remind one of the masks in *The Crimson Kimono* and fulfil a similar purpose.

Godard and Fuller use the genre, war movie or crime movie, only to destroy it by the urgency of the concerns they both pour into the form. Like *The Crimson Kimono*, *Pierrot le Fou* is a crime story which becomes a love story. *Made in USA* is about French politics just as *Underworld USA* is about American politics. Godard's interest in the inner lives and mutual conflicts of his protagonists pushes the mechanism of the thriller to the edges of the film, as Fuller does in *The Crimson Kimono*, so that the crime is used not as the driving force of the movie but as a comment on the personal problems of the protagonists.

Godard shares Fuller's distrust of totalitarianism in, for instance, *Les Carabiniers* and *Alphaville*. He also shares Fuller's distrust of his medium. Both combine documentary and fiction in an attempt to escape from the dream nature of the movies, and both use highly personal stories to comment on international political problems. Compare *Verboten* with *Deux ou Trois Choses*. Two highly didactic films, each presents a world of doomed individualists crushed by the comparable forces of right and left. *Made in USA* is rightly dedicated to Fuller. Karina, like Tolly Devlin or Spanier – Kenner, in her search for revenge is dragged ever deeper into a world of violent inter-totalitarian treachery. Like Lucky Legs she becomes involved in a political conflict that doesn't interest her; like Johnny Barrett her quest is really for the truth about herself as the identity of the man she seeks becomes ever more confused. Like Kelly in *The Naked Kiss*, Karina tries at the end to ride away from this irretrievably corrupt world. All Godard's characters, like O'Meara, are trying to escape to a better world, but a world which is shown to exist only in dreams: the vision of South America at the end of *Bande à Part*, Belmondo's desire to get to Rome in *Breathless*, Capri in *Contempt*, the South of France in *Pierrot le Fou*. The combined attraction and fear of the primitive in the end section of *Weekend* echoes the Sioux in *Run of the Arrow* and the nightmares in *Shock Corridor*.

Both directors use the prostitute to comment on the mercenary nature of modern life and as a symbol of the independent woman who does not become involved in the double-crosses of love. Compare Kelly and Lucky Legs with Karina in *Vivre Sa Vie* and Vlady in *Deux ou Trois Choses*.

The crucial difference between Godard and Fuller is one of pretension, of self-awareness. Fuller's films are more satisfying than Godard's because he is working within a healthier tradition. The stress in the European tradition upon the personal statement, and the alienation from the audience which the art-movie concept encourages, lead Godard to make evermore private statements. As Godard has tried to make his films more relevant in a direct political sense, they have, paradoxically, become increasingly indecipherable. Both Fuller and Godard are fascinated by journalism, although in Godard this fascination stems as much from Lang as from Fuller. Journalists and the ambience of journalism play a leading role in *Breathless*, *Le Petit Soldat*, *Une Femme Mariée*. Godard, like Fuller, worked as a journalist and scriptwriter before he became a director. Increasingly in Godard's movies this journalistic interest has turned in the direction of television current affairs and *cinéma vérité*. Both Godard and Fuller see films not as individual artefacts but as a continuous process. For Godard they are pages in a diary, for Fuller editions of a newspaper. While Fuller has been prepared to work within the limits of tabloid, mass-circulation journalism, Godard has increasingly tried to communicate through the equivalent of highly convoluted, cryptic, almost encoded articles in fringe left-wing magazines. Godard may intellectually admire Mao's Thoughts, but Fuller has the innocent courage actually to film in that sloganizing style. So while Fuller and Godard burst out of the limits of the genre, in Fuller's work the genre survives with sufficient strength and coherence to actively support the director's purposes. He can, in his own phrase, still tell a great yarn. *The Crimson Kimono* and *Underworld USA* still work as gangster pictures.

Filmography

Samuel Fuller

Born 12 August 1912 in Worcester, Massachusetts. From copy-boy to Arthur Brisbane on the *New York Journal*, became at seventeen the youngest crime reporter in New York. Travelled across the States covering trials, and wrote short stories and books for the rental trade (*Burn Baby Burn*, 1935; *Test Tube Baby* and *Make Up and Kiss*, 1936). Sold first script to Petroff in 1936. Started in the movie business around 1941. From call-up in 1942 served with the Sixteenth Company of the First US Infantry Division (known as 'The Big Red One') in North Africa and Sicily (where he won the Bronze Star); Normandy (Silver Star); Belgium, Germany and Czechoslovakia. In 1944, after leaving Army, wrote *The Dark Page*, selected by the Book Critics of America as the outstanding psychological novel of the year. (His screenplay of the book, first written for Howard Hawks, finally filmed as *Scandal Sheet*, 1952.) Started career as director with *I Shot Jesse James* (1948). Later novels include two based on movie scripts: *Shock Corridor* and *The Naked Kiss* (1963); and *Crown of India* (1966). Present book projects are *The Rifle*, dealing with Vietnam, and *144 Piccadilly*; possible films are *The Toy Soldiers* for producer Robert Cohn, and *The Kid From Soho* (Hemdale and Krofft Productions). Married Christa Lang, actress met in Paris, 1965. Has numerous projects for books, scripts and films.

Film appearances

In his own *House of Bamboo* (1955) as policeman – gets shot. Then in Godard's *Pierrot le Fou* (1965), Moullet's *Brigitte et Brigitte* (1966), and Dennis Hopper's *The Last Movie* (shot in Peru, 1970) – each time as himself.

TV Scripts

1962 *It Tolls For Thee* – episode of *The Virginian*; also a documentary dealing with narcotics.

1966 Five episodes of *The Iron Horse* – *The Man from Chicago*, *High Devil*, *Volcano Waggon*, *Hell Cat* and *Banner with a Strange Device*.

Movie stories and scripts

1936 *Hats Off* (director, Boris Petroff; script by Samuel Fuller and Edmund Joseph, from their original story, with additional dialogue by Thiele Lawrence).

1937 *It Happened in Hollywood/Once a Hero* (G.B. title) (director Harry Lachman; script by Ethel Hill, Harvey Ferguson and Samuel Fuller, from the story by Myles Connolly).

1938 *Gangs of New York* (director, James Cruze; script by Wellyn Tootman, Charles Francis Royal and Samuel Fuller, from a story by Samuel Fuller).

Adventure in Sahara (director, D. Ross Lederman; script by Maxwell Shane from a story by Samuel Fuller).

Federal Man-hunt (director, Nick Grinde; script by Maxwell Shane, from a story by Samuel Fuller and William Lively).

1940 *Bowery Boy* (director, William Morgan; script by Robert Chapin, Harry Kronman, Eugene Solow, from a story by Samuel Fuller and Sidney Sutherland).

1941 *Confirm or Deny* (directors, Archie Mayo, Fritz Lang; script by Jo Swerling, from the story by Henry Wales and Samuel Fuller).

1943 *The Power of the Press* (director, Lew Landers; script by Robert D. Andrews, from the story by Samuel Fuller (sold to Columbia 1938)).

1945 *Gangs of the Waterfront* (a remake of *Gangs of New York* 1938) (director, George Blair; script by Albert Bleich, from a story by Samuel Fuller).

1948 *Shockproof* (director, Douglas Sirk; script by Helen Deutsch, Samuel Fuller, from Fuller's story *The Lovers*. Fuller refuses to acknowledge any part in this film).

1951 *The Tanks are Coming* (director, Lewis Seiler; script by Robert Hardy Andrews, from a story by Samuel Fuller).

1952 *Scandal Sheet/The Dark Page* (G.B. title) (director, Phil Karlson; script by Ted Sherdeman, Eugene Ling, James Poe, from Samuel Fuller's novel *The Dark Page*).

1953 *The Command* (director, David Butler; script by Russell Hughes from the novel *The White Invader* by James Warner Bellah, adapted by Samuel Fuller. Because of changes to script, disclaimed by Fuller).

1968 *Cape Town Affair* (a remake of *Pickup on South Street*) (director, Robert Webb; script by Harold Medford and Samuel Fuller).

Features

I Shot Jesse James (1948)

Production Company	Lippert Productions for Screen Guild
Executive Producer	Robert L. Lippert
Producer	Carl K. Hittleman
Director	Samuel Fuller
Assistant Director	Johnny Grubbs

Script	Samuel Fuller, from an article by Homer Croy
Script Supervisor	Moree Herring
Director of Photography	Ernest Miller
Camera Operator	Archie Dalzell
Editor	Paul Landres
Art Director	Frank Hotaling
Set Decorators	John McCarthy, James Redd
Music	Albert Glasser
Song	Katherine Glasser

Preston Foster (*John Kelley*), Barbara Britton (*Cynthy Waters*), John Ireland (*Bob Ford*), Reed Hadley (*Jesse James*), J. Edward Bromberg (*Harry Kane*), Victor Kilian (*Soapy*), Barbara Woodell (*Mrs Zee James*), Tom Tyler (*Frank James*), Tom Noonan (*Charles Ford*), Byron Foulger (*Room Clerk*), Eddie Dunn (*Bartender*), Jeni Le Gon (*Maid*), Phil Pine (*Man in Saloon*), Robin Short (*Troubadour*), Margia Dean (*Singer in Bar*), Gene Collins (*Young Man who wants to kill Bob Ford*), Chuck Roberson (Double for Reed Hadley).

Filmed November 1948. Released in U.S.A., 26 February 1949; G.B., July 1949. Running time 81 min. (72 min. in G.B.).
Distributors: Screen Guild (U.S.A.), Exclusive (G.B.).
No longer available in G.B.

The Baron of Arizona (1949)

Production Company	Deputy Corp./ Lippert Productions
Producer	Carl K. Hittleman
Director	Samuel Fuller
Assistant Director	Frank Fox
Script	Samuel Fuller (from an article in *American Weekly*)*
Script Supervisor	Dorothy B. Cormack
Director of Photography	James Wong Howe
Camera Operator	Curt Fetters
Special Effects	Ray Mercer, Don Steward
Editor	Arthur Hilton
Art Director	P. Frank Sylos
Set Decorators	Otto Siegel, Ray Robinson
Music	Paul Dunlap
Costumes	Alfred Berke, Kitty Mayor

Vincent Price (*James Addison Reavis*), Ellen Drew (*Sofia Peralta-Reavis*), Beulah Bondi (*Lorna Morales*), Vladimir Sokoloff (*Pepito Alvarez*), Reed Hadley (*John Griff*), Robert Barratt (*Judge Adams*), Robin Short (*Lansing*),

Barbara Woodell (*Carry Lansing*), Tina Rome (*Rita*), Margia Dean (*Marquesa*), Edward Keane (*Surveyor Miller*), Gene Roth (*Father Guardian*), Karen Kester (*Sofia as a child*), Joseph Green (*Gunther*), Fred Kohler Jr (*Demming*), Tristram Coffin (*McCleary*), I. Stanford Jolley (*Secretary of the Interior*), Terry Frost (*Morelle*), Angelo Rosito (*Angie*), Zachery Yaconelli (*Greco*), Adolfo Ornelas (*Martinez*), Wheaton Chambers (*Brother Gregory*), Robert O'Neill (*Brother Paul*), Stephen Harrison (*Surveyor's Assistant*), Stuart Holmes (*Old Man hearing Reavis's story*), Jonathan Hale.

Filmed in 15 days, October–November 1949. Released in U.S.A., 4 March 1950; G.B., September 1950. Running time 97 min. (85 min. in G.B.). Distributors: Lippert (U.S.A.), Exclusive (G.B.). Current G.B. Distributor: Watso Films (16 mm.).

* Fuller's original script. *American Weekly* article used on credits for added prestige.

The Steel Helmet (1950)

Production Company	Deputy Corp./Lippert Productions
Executive Producer	Robert L. Lippert
Producer	Samuel Fuller
Associate Producer	William Berke
Director	Samuel Fuller
Assistant Director	John Francis Murphy
Script	Samuel Fuller
Director of Photography	Ernest W. Miller
Special Effects	Ben Southland, Ray Mercer
Editor	Philip Cahn
Art Director	Theobald Holsopple
Set Decorator	Clarence Steenson
Music	Paul Dunlap
Costumes	Alfred Berke

Gene Evans (*Sergeant Zack*), Robert Hutton (*Private 'Conchie' Bronte*), Richard Loo (*Sergeant 'Buddhahead' Tanaka*), Steve Brodie (*Lieutenant Driscoll*), James Edwards (*Corporal Thompson*), Sid Melton (*'Joe', Second GI*), Richard Monahan (*Private Baldy*), William Chun (*'Short Round'*), Harold Fong (*The Red*), Neyle Morrow (*First GI*), Lynn Stallmaster (*Second Lieutenant*).

Filmed in 10 days, October 1950. Released in U.S.A., 2 February 1951; G.B., 9 March 1951. Running time 84 min.

Distributors: Lippert (U.S.A.), Exclusive (G.B.).
Current G.B. Distributor: Watso Films (16 mm.).

Fixed Bayonets (1951)

Production Company	Twentieth Century Fox
Producer	Jules Buck
Director	Samuel Fuller
Assistant Director	Paul Melmick
Script	Samuel Fuller, from a novel by John Brophy*
Director of Photography	Lucien Ballard
Special Effects	Fred Sersen
Editor	Nick De Maggio
Art Directors	Lyle Wheeler, George Patrick
Set Decorators	Thomas Little, Fred J. Rhode
Music	Roy Webb
Musical Director	Lionel Newman
Orchestration	Maurice de Packh
Costumes	Charles Le Maire
Sound	Eugene Grossman, Harry M. Leonard
Technical Adviser	Captain Raymond Harvey

Richard Basehart (*Corporal Denno*), Gene Evans (*Sergeant Rock*), Michael O'Shea (*Sergeant Lonergan*), Richard Hylton (*Private Wheeler*), Craig Hill (*Lieutenant Gibbs*), Skip Homeier ('*Belvedere*' *Whitey*), Henry Kulky (*Vogl*), Richard Monahan (*Walowicz*), Paul Richards (*Ramirez*), Tony Kent (*Mainotes*), Don Orlando (*Borcellino*), Patrick Fitzgibbon (*Paddy*), Neyle Morrow (*Medic*), George Wesley (*Griff*), Mel Pogue (*Bulchek*), George Conrad (*Zablocki*), David Wolfson (*Bigmouth*), Buddy Thorpe (*Husky Doggie*), Al Negbo (*Lean Doggie*), Wyott Ordung (*Fitz*), Pat Hogan (*Jonesy*), James Dean (*GI*), John Doucette (*GI*), Bill Hickman, Kayne Shew.

Filmed on Stage 8, Twentieth Century Fox studio, July–August 1951. Released in U.S.A., December 1951; G.B., 15 March 1954. Running time 92 min.
Distributors: Twentieth Century Fox (U.S.A. and G.B.).
Current G.B. Distributor: F.D.A. (16 mm.).

* 'This was an original, but Darryl Zanuck decided to credit also an old film 20th made, *The Immortal Sergeant*, because it dealt with a timid soldier. The stories have nothing in common whatsoever.' (Samuel Fuller)

Park Row (1952)

Production Company	Samuel Fuller Productions for United Artists
Producer	Samuel Fuller
Production Supervisor	Sherman A. Harris
Director	Samuel Fuller
Assistant Director	Joseph Depew
Script	Samuel Fuller
Script Supervisor	Helen McCaffay
Director of Photography	Jack Russell
Special Effects	Roscoe S. Cline
Editor	Philip Cahn
Art Director	Theobald Holsopple
Set Decorator	Ray Robinson
Music	Paul Dunlap
Costumes	Jack Miller
Sound	Earl Crain Sr

Gene Evans (*Phineas Mitchell*), Mary Welch (*Charity Hackett*), Bela Kovacs (*Ottmar Mergenthaler*), Herbert Heyes (*Josiah Davenport*), Tina Rome (*Jenny O'Rourke*), George O'Hanlon (*Steve Brodie*), J. M. Kerrigan (*Dan O'Rourke*), Forrest Taylor (*Charles A. Leach*), Don Orlando (*Mr Angelo*), Neyle Morrow (*Thomas Guest*), Dick Elliott (*Jeff Hudson*), Stuart Randall (*Mr Spiro*), Dee Pollock (*Rusty*), Hal K. Dawson (*Mr Wiley*), Charles Horvath (*Man battered by Mitchell against monument*).

Filmed at General Service, January–February 1952. Released in U.S.A., 12 August 1952; G.B., December 1952. Running time 83 min.
Distributors: United Artists (U.S.A. and G.B.).
No longer available in G.B.

Pickup on South Street (1952)

Production Company	Twentieth Century Fox
Producer	Jules Schermer
Director	Samuel Fuller
Assistant Director	Ad Schaumer
Script	Samuel Fuller, from a story by Dwight Taylor*
Director of Photography	Joe MacDonald
Special Effects	Ray Kellogg
Editor	Nick De Maggio
Art Directors	Lyle Wheeler, George Patrick
Set Decorator	Al Orenbach

Music	Leigh Harline
Musical Director	Lionel Newman
Orchestration	Edward Powell
Costumes	Charles Le Maire, Travilla
Sound	Winston H. Leverett, Harry M. Leonard

Richard Widmark (*Skip McCoy*), Jean Peters (*Candy*), Thelma Ritter (*Moe Williams*), Murvyn Vye (*Captain Dan Tiger*), Richard Kiley (*Joey*), Willis B. Bouchey (*Zara*), Milburn Stone (*Wineki*), Henry Slate (*MacGregor*), Jerry O'Sullivan (*Enyart*), Harry Carter (*Dietrich*), George E. Stone (*Clerk, Police Station*), George Eldredge (*Fenton*), Stuart Randall (*Police Commissioner*), Frank Kumagi (*Lum*), Victor Perry (*Lightning Louie*), George Berkeley (*Customer*), Emmett Lynn (*Sandwich Man*), Maurice Samuels (*Peddler*), Parley Baer (*Stranger*), Jay Loftlin (*Librarian*), Virginia Carroll (*Nurse*), Roger Moore (*Mr Victor*).

Filmed on location in New York and Los Angeles; underground sequence under Twentieth Century Fox studio lot, September–October 1952. Released in U.S.A., June 1953; G.B., 10 August 1953. Running time 80 min. (77 min. in G.B.).

Distributors: Twentieth Century Fox (U.S.A. and G.B.).
Current G.B. Distributors: Twentieth Century Fox (35 mm.); Warner-Pathé (16 mm.).
Awarded Bronze Lion at the Venice Festival, 1953.

* 'Once again this was my original . . . Zanuck asked me to make *Blaze of Glory*, a script by Dwight Taylor . . . that triggered me to write an analytical assault of the mental and physical strength and weakness of a professional pickpocket. . . .' (Samuel Fuller)

Hell and High Water (1953)

Production Company	Twentieth Century Fox
Producer	Raymond A. Klune
Director	Samuel Fuller
Assistant Director	Ad Schaumer
Script	Jesse L. Lasky Jr and Samuel Fuller, from a story by David Hempstead
Director of Photography	Joe MacDonald
Colour Process	Technicolor
Colour Consultant	Leonard Doss
Special Effects	Ray Kellogg
Editor	James B. Clark
Art Directors	Lyle Wheeler, Leland Fuller
Set Decorators	Walter M. Scott, Stuart Reiss

Music	Alfred Newman
Orchestration	Edward B. Powell
Special Lyrics	Harry Powell
Costumes	Charles Le Maire, Travilla
Sound	Eugene Grossman, Roger Heman

Richard Widmark (*Adam Jones*), Bella Darvi (*Denise Gerard*), Victor Francen (*Professor Montel*), Cameron Mitchell ('*Ski*' *Brodski*), Gene Evans ('*Chief*' *Holter*), David Wayne (*Dugboat Walker*), Stephen Bekassy (*Neuman*), Richard Loo (*Fujimori*), Peter Scott (*Happy Mosk*), Henry Kulky (*Gunner McCrossin*), Wong Artane (*Chin Lee*), Harry Carter (*Quartermaster*), Robert Adler (*Welles*), Don Orlando (*Carpino*), Rollin Moriyama (*Joto*), John Gifford (*Torpedo*), William Yip (*Ho-Sin*), Tommy Walker (*Crew Member*), Leslie Bradley (*Mr Aylesworth*), John Weingraf (*Colonel Schuman*), Harry Denny (*McAuliff*), Edo Mita (*Taxi Driver*), Ramsey Williams (*Lieutenant*), Robert B. Williams (*Reporter*), Harlan Warde (*Photographer*), Neyle Morrow.

Filmed 60 days' shooting in submarine, 21 days studio, June–August 1953. ('We never went to sea on this sea film' (Samuel Fuller).) Released in U.S.A., February 1954; G.B., 7 June 1954. Running time 103 min. Distributors: Twentieth Century Fox (U.S.A. and G.B.). Current G.B. Distributor: Grand National (35 mm.).

House of Bamboo (1955)

Production Company	Twentieth Century Fox
Producer	Buddy Adler
Director	Samuel Fuller
Assistant Director	David Silver
Script	Harry Kleiner
Additional Dialogue	Samuel Fuller
Director of Photography	Joe MacDonald
Colour Process	Technicolor
Colour Consultant	Leonard Doss
Special Effects	Ray Kellogg
Editor	James B. Clark
Art Directors	Lyle Wheeler, Addison Hehr
Set Decorators	Walter M. Scott, Stuart Reiss
Music	Leigh Harline
Musical Director	Lionel Newman
Orchestration	Edward B. Powell
Song 'House of Bamboo'	Leigh Harline, Jack Brooks
Costumes	Charles Le Maire

Robert Ryan (*Sandy Dawson*), Robert Stack (*Eddie Spanier/Sergeant Kenner*), Shirley Yamaguchi (*Mariko*), Cameron Mitchell (*Griff*), Brad Dexter (*Captain Hanson*), Sessue Hayakawa (*Inspector Kita*), Biff Elliott (*Webber*), Sandro Giglio (*Ceran*), Elko Hanabusa (*Japanese Screaming Woman*), Harry Carey (*John*), Peter Gray (*Willy*), Robert Quarry (*Phil*), DeForest Kelley (*Charlie*), John Doucette (*Skipper*), Teru Shimada (*Nagaya*), Robert Hosoi (*Doctor*), Jack Maeshiro (*Bartender*), May Takasugi (*Bath Attendant*), Robert Okazaki (*Mr Hommaru*), Barry Coe (*Hanson's Deputy*), Neyle Morrow (*Corporal Davis*), Reiko Hayakawa (*Mariko's Girl friend*), Sandy Ozeka (*Sandy's 'Kimono Girl'*), Samuel Fuller (*Policeman*), with the Shochiku Troupe from Kokusai Theatre.

Filmed on location in Tokyo and Yokohama, February–March 1955. Released in U.S.A., July 1955; G.B., 21 November 1955. Running time 102 min.
Distributors: Twentieth Century Fox (U.S.A. and G.B.).
Current G.B. Distributor: Ron Harris (16 mm.).

Run of the Arrow (1956)

Production Company	Globe Enterprises for R.K.O., released by Universal
Producer	Samuel Fuller
Production Manager	Gene Bryant
Director	Samuel Fuller
Assistant Director	Ben Chapman
Script	Samuel Fuller
Director of Photography	Joseph Biroc
Colour Process	Technicolor
Editor	Gene Fowler Jr
Art Directors	Albert D'Agostino, Jack Okey
Set Decorator	Bert Granger
Music	Victor Young
Sound	Virgil Smith

Rod Steiger (*O'Meara*), Sarita Montiel (*Yellow Moccasin*), Brian Keith (*Captain Clark*), Ralph Meeker (*Lieutenant Driscoll*), Jay C. Flippen (*Walking Coyote*), Charles Bronson (*Blue Buffalo*), Olive Carey (*Mrs O'Meara*), H.M. Wynant (*Crazy Wolf*), Neyle Morrow (*Lieutenant Stockwell*), Frank de Kova (*Red Cloud*), Stuart Randall (*Colonel Taylor*), Colonel Tim McCoy (*General Allen*), Frank Warner (*Ballad Singer*), Billy Miller (*Silent Tongue*), Chuck Hayward (*Corporal*), Carleton Young

(*Doctor*), Chuck Roberson (*Sergeant*); (Angie Dickinson dubbed Sarita Montiel).

Filmed on location at St George, Utah, June–July 1956. Released in U.S.A., September 1957; G.B., 4 November 1957. Running time 86 min.
Distributors: Universal (U.S.A.), R.K.O. (G.B.).
Current G.B. Distributor: Robert Kingston Films (16 mm.).

China Gate (1957)

Production Company	Globe Enterprises for Twentieth Century Fox
Producer	Samuel Fuller
Production Manager	William J. Magginetti
Director	Samuel Fuller
Assistant Director	Harold E. Knox
Script	Samuel Fuller
Director of Photography	Joseph Biroc
Special Effects	Norman Breedlove, Linwood Dunn
Editors	Gene Fowler Jr, Dean Harrison
Art Director	John Mansbridge
Set Decorator	Glen Daniels
Music	Victor Young 'extended by his old friend Max Steiner'
Music Editor	Audrey Granville
Song 'China Gate'	Victor Young, Harold Adamson, sung by Nat 'King' Cole
Costumes	Henry West, Beau Van den Ecker
Sound	Jean Speak
Supervising Sound Editor	Bert Schoenfield

Gene Barry (*Brock*), Angie Dickinson (*Lia 'Lucky Legs' Surmer*), Nat 'King' Cole (*Goldie*), Paul Dubov (*Captain Caumont*), Lee Van Cleef (*Major Cham*), George Givot (*Corporal Pigalle*), Gerald Milton (*Private Andreades*), Neyle Morrow (*Leung*), Marcel Dalio (*Father Paul*), Maurice Marsac (*Colonel De Sars*), Warren Hsieh (*Boy*), Paul Busch (*Corporal Kruger*), Sasha Harden (*Private Jaszi*), James Hong (*Charlie*), William Soo Hoo (*Guard* and *Moi Leader*), Weaver Levy (*Khuan*), Ziva Rodann (*Indo-Chinese*).

Filmed at R.K.O.-Pathé, January 1957. Released in U.S.A., May 1957; G.B., 8 July 1957. Running time 97 min. (90 min. in G.B.).
Distributors: Twentieth Century Fox (U.S.A. and G.B.).
Current G.B. Distributor: Twentieth Century Fox.

Forty Guns (1957)

Production Company	Globe Enterprises for Twentieth Century Fox
Producer	Samuel Fuller
Director	Samuel Fuller
Assistant Director	Harold E. Knox
Script	Samuel Fuller
Director of Photography	Joseph Biroc
Special Effects	Norman Breedlove, L. B. Abbott, Linwood Dunn
Editor	Gene Fowler Jr
Art Director	John Mansbridge
Set Decorators	Walter M. Scott, Chester Bayhi
Music	Harry Sukman
Songs 'High Ridin' Woman'	Harold Adamson, Harry Sukman
'God Has His Arms Around me'	Harold Adamson, Victor Young
Costumes	Charles Le Maire, Leah Rhodes
Sound	Jean Speak, Harry M. Leonard

Barbara Stanwyck (*Jessica Drummond*), Barry Sullivan (*Griff Bonnell*), Dean Jagger (*Ned Logan*), John Ericson (*Brock Drummond*), Gene Barry (*Wes Bonnell*), Robert Dix (*Chico Bonnell*), 'Jidge' Carroll (*Barney Cashman*), Paul Dubov (*Judge Macy*), Gerald Milton (*Shotgun Spanger*), Ziva Rodann (*Rio*), Hank Worden (*John Chisum*), Sandra Wirth (*Chico's Girlfriend*), Neyle Morrow (*Wiley*), Eve Brent (*Louvenia Spanger*), Chuck Roberson (*Swain*), Chuck Hayward (*Charlie Savage*).

Filmed April–May 1957. Released in U.S.A., September 1957; G.B., 17 October 1957. Running time 80 min.
Distributors: Twentieth Century Fox (U.S.A. and G.B.).
No longer available in G.B.

Verboten (1958)

Production Company	Globe Enterprises for R.K.O., released by Columbia
Producer	Samuel Fuller
Production Manager	Walter Daniels
Director	Samuel Fuller
Assistant Director	Gordon McLean
Script	Samuel Fuller
Director of Photography	Joseph Biroc
Camera Operator	William Cline
Special Effects	Norman Breedlove

Editor	Philip Cahn
Art Director	John Mansbridge
Set Decorator	Glen L. Daniels
Music	Harry Sukman; themes from Wagner and Beethoven
Costumes	Bernice Pontrelli, Harry West
Sound	Bert Schoenfeld, Jean Speak
Technical Adviser	Commandant Raymond Harvey

James Best (*Sergeant David Brent*), Susan Cummings (*Helga Schiller*), Tom Pittman (*Bruno Eckart*), Paul Dubov (*Captain Harvey*), Harold Daye (*Franz*), Dick Kallman (*Helmuth*), Stuart Randall (*Colonel*), Steven Geray (*Bürgermeister*), Anna Hope (*Frau Schiller*), Robert Boon (*SS Officer*), Sasha Harden (*Erich*), Paul Busch (*Guenther*), Neyle Morrow (*Sergeant Kellogg*), Joseph Turkel (*Infantryman*), Charles Horvath (*Man whose daughter has head shaved*).

Filmed April–May 1958. Released in U.S.A., May 1959; G.B., 23 June 1959. Running time 94 min. (86 min. in G.B.).
Distributors: Columbia (U.S.A.), Rank (G.B.).
Current G.B. Distributor: Robert Kingston Films (16 mm.).

The Crimson Kimono (1959)

Production Company	Globe Enterprises for Columbia
Producer	Samuel Fuller
Director	Samuel Fuller
Assistant Director	Floyd Joyer
Script	Samuel Fuller
Director of Photography	Sam Leavitt
Editor	Jerome Thoms
Art Directors	William E. Flannery, Robert Boyle
Set Decorator	James Crowe
Music	Harry Sukman
Orchestration	Leo Shuken, Jack Hayes
Costumes	Bernice Pontrelli
Sound	Josh Westmoreland
Sound Recording Supervisor	John Livadry

James Shigeta (*Detective Joe Kojaku*), Glenn Corbett (*Detective Sergeant Charlie Bancroft*), Victoria Shaw (*Christine Downes*), Anna Lee (*Mac*), Paul Dubov (*Casale*), Jaclynne Greene (*Roma Wilson*), Neyle Morrow (*Hansel*), Gloria Pall (*Sugar Torch*), Barbara Hayden (*Mother*), George Yoshinaga (*Willy Hidaka*), Kaye Elhardt (*Nun*), Aya Oyama (*Sister Gertrude*), George Okamura (*Karate*), Rev. Ryosho S. Sogabe (*Priest*), Robert Okazaki (*Yoshinaga*), Fuji (*Shuto*), Walter Burke.

Filmed, partly on location in Los Angeles' 'Little Tokyo', February–
March 1959. Released in U.S.A., October 1959; G.B., 25 April 1960.
Running time 82 min.
Distributors: Columbia (U.S.A. and G.B.).
Current G.B. Distributor: Columbia.

Underworld USA (1960)

Production Company	Globe Enterprises for Columbia
Producer	Samuel Fuller
Director	Samuel Fuller
Assistant Director	Floyd Joyer
Script	Samuel Fuller, based on articles by Joseph F. Dineen★
Director of Photography	Hal Mohr
Editor	Jerome Thoms
Art Director	Robert Peterson
Set Decorator	Bill Calvert
Music	Harry Sukman
Costumes	Bernice Pontrelli
Sound	Charles J. Rice
Sound Recording Supervisor	Josh Westmoreland

Cliff Robertson (*Tolly Devlin*), Beatrice Kay (*Sandy*), Larry Gates
(*Driscoll*), Richard Rust (*Gus*), Dolores Dorn (*Cuddles*), Robert Emhardt
(*Connors*), Paul Dubov (*Gela*), Gerald Milton (*Gunther*), Allan Greuner
(*Smith*), David Kent (*Tolly as a Boy*), Neyle Morrow (*Barney*), Henry
Norell (*Prison Doctor*), Sally Mills (*Connie*), Tina Rome (*Woman*), Robert
P. Lieb (*Officer*), Peter Brocco (*Vic Farrar*).

Filmed July–August 1960. Released in U.S.A., March 1961; G.B., August
1962. Running time 98 min. (95 min. in G.B.).
Distributors: Columbia (U.S.A. and G.B.).
Current G.B. Distributor: Columbia.

★Fuller's original. *Saturday Evening Post* article 'Underworld U.S.A.'
bought for the title.

Merrill's Marauders (1961)

Production Company	United States Productions for Warner Brothers
Producer	Milton Sperling
Production Supervisor	William Magginetti
Director	Samuel Fuller
Assistant Director	William Kissel

Script	Samuel Fuller, Milton Sperling from the novel by Charlton Ogburn Jr
Director of Photography	William Clothier
Colour Process	Technicolor
Special Effects	Ralph Ayres
Editor	Folmar Blangsted
Art Director	William Magginetti
Music	Howard Jackson
Sound	Francis M. Stahl
Technical Adviser	Lieutenant-Colonel Samuel Wilson

Jeff Chandler (*Brigadier-General Frank Merrill*), Ty Hardin (*Lieutenant Lee Stockton*), Peter Brown (*Bullseye*), Andrew Duggan (*Major 'Doc' Nemeny*), Will Hutchins (*Chowhound*), Claud Akins (*Sergeant Kolowicz*), Luz Valdez (*Burmese Girl*), John Hoyt (*General 'Vinegar Joe' Stilwell*), Charles Briggs (*Muley*), Chuck Roberson (*American Officer* and *Japanese Guard*), Chuck Hayward (*Officer*), Jack C. Williams (*Medic*), Chuck Hicks (*Corporal Doskis*), Vaughan Wilson (*Lieutenant-Colonel Bannister*), Pancho Magolona (*Taggy*).

Filmed on location in the Philippines, March–May 1961. Released in U.S.A., 7 July 1962; G.B., 9 July 1962. Running time 98 min. (91 min. in G.B.).
Distributors: Warners (U.S.A. and G.B.).
Current G.B. Distributor: Warner-Pathé (16 mm.).

Shock Corridor (1963)

Production Company	Fromkess-Firks for Allied Artists
Producer	Samuel Fuller
Production Manager	Randolph Flothow
Director	Samuel Fuller
Assistant Director	Floyd Joyer
Script	Samuel Fuller from his scenario *Strait-jacket*
Director of Photography	Stanley Cortez
Special Effects	Lynn Dunn
Editor	Jerome Thoms
Art Director	Eugene Lourie
Set Decorator	Charles Thompson
Music	Paul Dunlap
Costumes	Einar H. Bourman
Choreography	John Gregory
Sound	Phil Mitchel

Peter Breck (*Johnny Barrett*), Constance Towers (*Cathy*), Gene Evans (*Boden*), James Best (*Stuart*), Hari Rhodes (*Trent*), Larry Tucker (*Pagliacci*), William Zuckert (*Swanee*), Philip Ahn (*Dr Fong*), John Mathews (*Dr Cristo*), Neyle Morrow (*Psycho*), Chuck Roberson (*Wilkes*), John Craig (*Lloyd*), Frankie Gerstle (*Police Lieutenant*), Paul Dubov (*Dr Menkin*), Rachel Romen (*Singing Nympho*), Linda Randolph (*Dance Teacher*), Marie Devereux (*Nympho*), Lucille Curtis, Wally Campo, Karen Conrad, Barbara Perry, Marlene Manners, Jeanette Dana, Allison Daniell, Chuck Hicks, Ray Baxter, Linda Barrett, Harry Fleer.

Filmed in studio, February–March 1963 (hallucination sequences from film shot by Fuller while on location for *House of Bamboo*, plus scenes shot in Matto Grosso, Brazil while on location for *Tigrero* (unfinished film)). Released in U.S.A., 18 September 1963; G.B., London release 30 April 1970. Running time 101 min.
Distributors: Allied Artists (U.S.A.), Amanda Films (G.B.).
Current G.B. Distributor: Amanda Films (35 and 16 mm.).

The Naked Kiss (1963)

Production Company	Fromkess-Firks for Allied Artists
Executive Producers	Leo Fromkess, Sam Firks
Producer	Samuel Fuller
Production Manager	Herbert G. Luft
Director	Samuel Fuller
Assistant Director	Nate Levinson
Script	Samuel Fuller
Director of Photography	Stanley Cortez
Camera Operator	Frank Dugas
Editor	Jerome Thoms
Art Director	Eugene Lourie
Set Decorator	Victor Gangelin
Music	Paul Dunlap
Song 'Santa Lucia'	Sung by John Guarniere
Costumes	Act III, Einar H. Bourman
Sound	Alfred J. Overton

Constance Towers (*Kelly*), Anthony Eisley (*Griff*), Michael Dante (*Grant*), Virginia Grey (*Candy*), Patsy Kelly (*Mac*), Betty Bronson (*Miss Josephine*), Marie Devereux (*Buff*), Karen Conrad (*Dusty*), Linda Francis (*Rembrandt*), Barbara Perry (*Edna*), Walter Mathews (*Mike*), Betty Robinson (*Bunny*), Gerald Michenaud (*Kip*), Christopher Barry (*Peanuts*), George Spell (*Tim*), Patty Robinson (*Angel Face*), Neyle Morrow (*Officer Sam*), Monte Mansfield (*Farlunde*), Fletcher Fist (*Barney*), Gerald Milton (*Zookie*),

Breena Howard (*Redhead*), Sally Mills (*Marshmallow*), Edy Williams (*Hatrack*), Michael Barrere (*Young Delinquent*), Patricia Gayle (*Nurse*), Sheila Mintz (*Receptionist*), Bill Sampson (*Jerry*), Charlie (*Charlie*).

Filmed October–November 1963. Venice scenes taken from 16-mm. footage made in 1954. Released in U.S.A., 1 May 1964; G.B., London release 30 April 1970. Running time 93 min.
Distributors: Allied Artists (U.S.A.), Amanda Films (G.B.).
Current G.B. Distributor: Amanda Films (35 and 16 mm.).

Shark/Caine (1969)★

Production Company	Heritage/Calderon
Producers	Skip Steloff, Mark Cooper, Jose Luis Calderon
Director	Samuel Fuller★
Script	Samuel Fuller from the novel by Victor Canning★

Burt Reynolds (*Caine*), Barry Sullivan (*Mallare*), Arthur Kennedy (*Doctor*), Silvia Pinal (*Woman*), Enrique Lucero (*Policeman*).

Filmed in Mexico at Vera Cruz, Manzanillo.

★'I asked my name to be taken off . . . producer refused. . . . I want no credit for this film or mention in connection with it since it is not my film.' (Samuel Fuller)

Acknowledgements

I should like to thank the organizers of the Fuller Retrospective at the Edinburgh Film Festival 1969, and especially Murray Grigor, for their help and hospitality. In the realm of ideas, I am particularly indebted to the criticism of Victor Perkins and Peter Wollen. I should like to thank the staff of the NFT for enabling me to see and re-see Fuller's movies, and the staff of the BFI for their help with the stills and filmography. Finally, my gratitude to Sam Fuller for providing stills and answering countless questions.

Stills are reproduced by courtesy of: Samuel Fuller (from his own collection); Amanda Films (*Shock Corridor* and *The Naked Kiss*); Columbia (*The Crimson Kimono* and *Underworld USA*); Gerald A. Fernback Associates (*Run of the Arrow* and *Verboten*); Twentieth Century Fox (*China Gate*, *Fixed Bayonets*, *Hell and High Water* and *House of Bamboo*); Warner Pathé (*Merrill's Marauders* and *Pickup on South Street*); and Watsofilms Ltd (*The Baron of Arizona* and *The Steel Helmet*).